Hawley Smart

Saddle and Sabre

A Novel: Vol. I.

Hawley Smart

Saddle and Sabre
A Novel: Vol. I.

ISBN/EAN: 9783337031510

Printed in Europe, USA, Canada, Australia, Japan

Cover: Foto ©Andreas Hilbeck / pixelio.de

More available books at **www.hansebooks.com**

SADDLE AND SABRE.

A Novel.

BY

HAWLEY SMART

AUTHOR OF "BREEZIE LANGTON," "FROM POST TO FINISH,"
"BAD TO BEAT," ETC. ETC.

IN THREE VOLUMES.

VOL. I.

LONDON : CHAPMAN AND HALL
LIMITED
1888

WESTMINSTER:
PRINTED BY NICHOLS AND SONS,
25, PARLIAMENT STREET.

CONTENTS OF VOL. I.

CHAPTER XI.

CHAPTER XII.

CHAPTER XIII.

CHAPTER XIV.

CHAPTER XV.

CHAPTER XVI.

SADDLE AND SABRE.

CHAPTER I.

NORTH LEACH.

NESTLING at the foot of one of the long undulations of the Lincolnshire wolds stood a large, many-gabled, irregular house, a house wont to puzzle the traveller as to what manner of man might be its owner. It was too big for a farmhouse, nor did it look in the least like a rectory; moreover, nothing stood near it but some three or four labourers' cottages. As you looked closer you became conscious that the central

portion was most substantially built, and
evidently of older date than the wings,
which had apparently been added to it later.
One peculiarity about it, rather striking in a
house of this size, was that it was thatched,
neatly and very trimly thatched, no doubt,
but still that was a roof you would have
hardly expected to find on a house of this
class. North Leach, as the place was
called, had been the home of the Devereuxes
for certainly something like four centuries.
There they had farmed some four hundred
acres of their own so successfully that they
had now for many years rented an adjoining
farm of some seven or eight hundred acres,
a property of the great territorial magnate
of that part of Lincolnshire. This was
farming on a large scale; but, although the
times were not so prosperous for agricul-
turists as during the days of the tremendous
struggle with Napoleon, still things were
very flourishing. The farmers, albeit the
Corn Laws had been repealed, made money

hand over hand, and lived royally. Old
Tom Devereux kept so many horses of one
kind and another at North Leach that
gossip had it that Mrs. Devereux was always
asked whether she would have four greys,
browns, chestnuts, or what not, for Doncaster
races, a festival which the Devereuxes had
attended with the utmost regularity for
many years.

The present generation of the family had
been brought up in very different fashion
from their predecessors. Both sons had
been to Cambridge, while Lettice Devereux
had acquired everything that masters and a
fashionable school could teach her. As for
riding, there never was a Devereux that
could not ride. Both the men and women
of the family were thoroughly at home in
the saddle, and well-known as amongst the
best and boldest riders with the Brocklesby.
In front of the house, indeed running
round three sides of it, and just beyond
the gardens and shrubberies which imme-

diately surrounded it, was what was called
" the paddock," a large grass-field of about
fifty acres, virgin turf which had never
known the ploughshare. Along one side of
it were various artificial fences, such as are
used for schooling purposes; for the making
of hunters was always being pursued at
North Leach with great assiduity. Neither
Tom Devereux nor his sons could be correctly designated horse-dealers, but when
you have such a quantity of horses as were
required for the work of a farm, to say
nothing of a long string of hunters and
carriage-horses, it stands to reason that
there must necessarily be a good deal of
buying and selling connected with the
establishment. Further, there were a few
brood-mares at North Leach, and, consequently, a certain amount of young stock,
some of which usually had to be disposed
of. There was one thing certain at the big
farm, they could utilise horseflesh in a great
number of ways, and if a horse gave no

promise of making a hunter there were
many other paths in life to which he could
be introduced.

Inside, the house was, as might be expected, a roomy, comfortable old building,
·hich had been most judiciously modern-
ised. In the central, or original house, so
to speak, the rooms were low, with black
oak paneling, and floors to match; but in
the wings the rooms were far more lofty,
and a very pleasant drawing-room in the
one wing was balanced by an equally comfortable billiard-room on the other side of
the hall.

At the time my story opens, John Devereux, the eldest son, had left the University
some two years, and had steadily settled
down as his father's partner: not but what
old Tom Devereux was a hale, hearty man
of his years yet; but men do not, as a rule,
ride quite so hard to hounds at sixty as
they do in the days of their hot youth.
We all learn to take our pleasures more

soberly, and it is well for us, too, if we can
take our work somewhat more leisurely.
The overlooking of two such farms as North
Leach and the adjacent one, held upon
lease, involves a considerable amount of
hard work, and Tom Devereux was well-
pleased when his son settled down to follow
steadily in his footsteps. There had been
times when he had somewhat doubted the
wisdom of having allowed his sons to go to
the University—at all events, the eldest;
he had been afraid it might unsettle him,
and give him a distaste for the calling of a
yeoman farmer; and then the old man had
thought solemnly of what was to become of
the land if there was no one to take his
place when he was gone. He was fond of
the old acres that had come down to him
through so many generations of Devereux.
He had made his money out of the land,
and respected it accordingly. Moreover, he
was as honestly proud and fond of the old
home of his family as any noble in the land

could be of the stately mansion transmitted to him through a long line of ancestors.

A grey November day is closing in as Lettice Devereux enters the drawing-room, and promptly rings for tea. She is soon seated in a comfortable armchair in front of the glowing fire, in lazy enjoyment of that luxury. A sharp gallop with the hounds that morning has induced a pleasant languor, which, now that she has changed her dress, she feels justified in indulging in. She is already half-asleep, when the door opens abruptly, and her brother, in well-splashed boots and well-stained pink, enters the room.

"Holloa, Lettice," he exclaimed, "what became of you? You didn't come to grief of any kind with the young one, did you? But I missed you just after that rattling burst we had in the morning; and though we were lucky enough to find an afternoon fox, who gave us a very decent run, I never caught sight of your habit again."

"No, John," rejoined the girl laughing, "and I will tell you why. That four-year-old has the makings of as good a hunter as we have got in the stable. He carried me beautifully, and made never a mistake at his fences all the morning. But, when we trotted off to look for that second fox, he began to blunder a good deal. And the reason was obvious, the horse was tired; quite reason enough for taking him home. We all know nothing breaks the heart of a young one so much as asking him to go on when he is tired."

"Ah! you really think well of the young one then, do you?" said John Devereux with evident interest, as he sipped his tea.

"I do," replied Lettice, "and, what is more, I have an idea that he has a great turn of speed. I think it would be quite worth your while at the end of the hunting-season to try him. I think you will find that he is rather above hunter class."

"We shall see," replied John. "Anyway,

your schooling will go a great way towards the completion of his education. Have you heard from Charlie, and when he is coming down?"

"Next week. Do you know anything of this Mr. Furzedon that he is bringing with him ?"

"No. You see, although Charlie and I certainly just were together at Cambridge, I was a good bit before his time. I was leaving just as he came up, and during the term we were there together our sets were very different. As for this fellow, Furzedon, I never heard of him, but he is evidently a great pal of Charlie's; at all events he can ride a bit, and therefore we shall have no trouble about making him happy here, as long as the horses hold out; and, if he wants a breather after partridges, goodness knows we're plenty of them, although it takes hard walking to pick up a few brace now."

"I've no doubt we can make it pleasant enough for Mr. Furzedon," rejoined Lettice.

" I am bound to say that most of the friends
you and Charlie ask here generally seem
excessively pleased with the amusements we
provide for them, and I have very little
doubt Mr. Furzedon will fall into our
grooves quite as naturally as the rest of
them."

" Well, now I'm off," rejoined John
Devereux, " to exchange my dirty boots,
&c., for more civilised garments." And so
saying, he left his sister to enjoy her second
cup of tea, and indulge in dreamy reflection.

Miss Devereux was so far very well satisfied with her lot in life. A high-spirited girl
of twenty, disposed to make the best of
everything, she found her home-life very
enjoyable. There was always plenty to
amuse her about the farm, and, although
North Leach was rather an isolated resi-
dence, yet people in those parts had generally full stables, and made little of distances, and thought nothing of a ten or
twelve mile drive to a country ball, or other

revel. Balls, it is true, were not very numerous; but then Lettice, though she could
throw her heart and soul into a dance, was
by no means hungry for such entertainments.
As for the winter time, the prevalent feeling
in those parts was, as Whyte Melville puts
it, that "the business of life was to hunt
every day;" and Lettice dearly loved a good
gallop. As she sat lazily there in front of
the fire, she was speculating a good deal on
the return of her favourite brother. She
was very fond of John, but his quiet, sedate
manner did not accord with her own mirth-
loving nature, like Charlie's. John was some
six or seven years older than herself, but
might have been, from the grave, serious
way in which he took both his work and his
pleasure, a score of years her senior. It was
difficult to work John up to great enthusiasm
about anything; his cool head never seemed
to lose its balance for one moment; such
high spirits as at times possessed herself and
Charlie never ran away with John. She did

not trouble her head very much about this
Mr. Furzedon, although her brother had been
very full of him during the last few months.
Truth to tell, she was thinking more about
how well her horse had carried her than
anything else.

Sitting in the sitting-room of a quiet
lodging in Duke Street, smoking a short pipe,
was a fair-haired blue-eyed young fellow,
gazing into the fire, and evidently deeply
absorbed in thought—thoughts not of the
pleasantest, apparently, to judge from the
knit brows and somewhat serious aspect of
the young face.

"What an ass I have been," muttered
Charlie Devereux as he puffed savagely at
his pipe. "I wish to Heaven I'd never let
Furzedon persuade me to go to Newmarket.
I have had a bet before, of course, but I
never went regularly in for it till this time,
and three such meetings as I've had are
enough to break any one; indeed, if it hadn't
been for Furzedon's help, I should have been

unable to settle. Bad form, too, borrowing money from a pal, and, as to paying him, there's only one thing for it. I must sell the hunters. It is rough, but, as he is coming down to North Leach to hunt with me, I suppose he'll let me have two or three months of them before the sacrifice. However, even then, if I'm bid a good price I shall have to take it. I wonder whether they have anything at home they will let me have the riding of."

None knew better than Charlie that the big London dealers always had their eye upon North Leach. Many a letter did Tom Devereux get in the course of the season to know whether he had a hunter or two that he was disposed to part with. The dealers knew very well that when a horse from North Leach was guaranteed a made hunter, they could perfectly rely that it was so. And for an animal of that description a London dealer invariably has a market. There are plenty of his wealthy customers

who would always sooner trust to his judgment than their own, and have no objection
to pay the extra price.

" Well," thought Charlie with all the
elasticity of youth, " it will be very jolly to
have a real good gossip with Lettice, and to
have a good time with the Brocklesbys. I
never think hunting so good anywhere as it
is in my 'ain countree.' " Here his re-
flections were interrupted by a sharp knock
at the door, and the appearance of a tall
dark young man, with a florid countenance
and slightly Semitic nose.

" What, Charlie, all in the downs ! " he
said; " what nonsense ! It is no use being
down in your luck because you've had a
facer, besides, it's all squared up now. Let's
dine together, have a bottle of champagne,
and then go off to the theatre. I've got all
my business done in London, and am good to
go down to North Leach with you whenever
you like, and what's more we ought not to
lose such beautifully open weather as this."

So the two dined at Limmer's, and the bottle of champagne, as was only natural, expanded into two, and then they adjourned to the Strand Theatre, and were convulsed with laughter at one of the burlesques which characterised those palmy days of the Strand. I am writing of a good many years ago, when night-houses existed in the Haymarket, and in pursuit of that very questionable experience, the seeing of life, it was deemed incumbent on the young men of the day to drop into two or three before returning home. Inferior alcohol, and the most dubious company, male and female, was all the entertainment that these dens afforded, but then it was the proper thing to do, and in our younger days there are very few of us who do not deem that sufficient reason for the committal of any absurdity.

Furzedon and Charlie Devereux, of course, thought it necessary to have a lobster or some oysters at one of these houses, and, as they sallied out after having their supper, a dilapidated man suddenly exclaimed : " Ah, Furzedon—I beg pardon, Mr. Furzedon— you're good I'm sure to stand a sovereign to an old pal who is down in his luck."

Furzedon's eyes gleamed dangerously in the gaslight for a moment as he retorted in stern measured tones, " I don't know who you are, but I do know that you'll get never a sixpence from me to-night."

" D'ye hear him, mates ? " replied the dilapidated one, addressing some three or four similar birds of ill-omen, who were hanging about the entrance of the house in question. " Pretty conduct this to expect from a fellow who was your intimate friend, and for whom you did some tolerably dirty work no very short time ago."

" Shame, shame!" cried the ragged chorus, " why don't you stand to the gentleman now he is down in his luck ? " Keenly alive, these supporters of the sturdy mendicant, to the probability of " glasses round," should he succeed in extorting that sovereign from the " swell."

" Close up, Charlie," said Furzedon in a low voice, " these curs are going to rush us, and see what they can make in turning our pockets out. Just follow my lead. As soon as that scoundrel comes up with his whining petition again, I shall let him have it hot. Hit out at once all you know, and we shall be through them and into a hansom in less than two minutes. In the meantime do as I do." And Mr. Furzedon rapidly buttoned his overcoat up tightly. Another moment, and the suppliant for relief advanced with an impudent leer, and said, " Come, Mr. Furzedon, we don't part like this; I'm not going to want a sovereign while your pockets are well lined."

" Ah! you think so," replied Furzedon, with a low laugh. " I told you you should get nothing from me to-night. I lied; you shall," and, taking a step forward, Furzedon let go his left straight and true from the

shoulder, and stretched the luckless mendicant well-nigh senseless on the pavement.
There was a rapid rush of his companions,
but the quick, straight, determined hitting
of Furzedon and Charlie speedily dissipated
that attempt at plunder, and in another
minute the pair were driving rapidly home
to their lodgings in Duke Street.

Nothing perhaps in the episode of a mere
night-row in the Haymarket to influence
the destiny of anybody connected with this
history, and yet it is these very small events
that so often bear curiously upon our lives.
Had Furzedon given the unfortunate out-
cast of the Haymarket a sovereign, instead
of a blow, it would probably have made a
considerable difference in the course of his
life.

CHAPTER II.

MAJOR BRADDOCK'S DINNER.

THE strangers' room at the Thermopolium
was very full, and there was much talk and
laughter going on at the various little tables
as the wine passed merrily round them; but,
perhaps, from none did the laughter ripple
more freely than from a round table in the
middle of the room, around which half-a-
dozen men were gathered, the guests of jolly
Major Braddock. The Major was in his
element; he was never more happy than
when giving a little dinner; he flattered
himself that he knew how to do it, and,
what was more to the point, he did. Looking at his rubicund face and portly figure,

c 2

it was difficult now to imagine the Major a
smart officer of Hussars, and yet, ten years
before, when he finally doffed the pelisse, he
was as good-looking a dragoon as ever wore
sabretache.

But a man naturally a *bon vivant* gives
himself free licence in the matter of good
living, and who is not given in any way to
field-sports, rapidly puts on weight after he
has turned thirty. The Major was comfortably off, and when he sold out subsided at
once into a man about town. The giving
and partaking of little dinners entered prominently into the scheme of his life, and it
was now well known that an invitation from
Bob Braddock was not a thing to be lightly
declined; nor, on the other hand, was he a
man to whom an invitation was to be lightly
issued. It was understood through Clubland
that Bob Braddock's verdict on a dinner
was unimpeachable, and there were some
one or two of those monachal institutions
which he specially tabooed, saying that it

was a positive insult to ask any thing but
a raw boy to partake of food within their
gates while they kept such an atrocious
cook."

"Ha-ha!" laughed the Major, and it was
one of those mellow laughs which almost
instinctively carried the hearers away with
it. "What times those were! What con-
stitutions we all had in those days, and,
Heaven help us, how shamefully ignorant we
were on the subject of wine and cookery!
Just you try that champagne, Norman.
Here, waiter, get Mr. Slade a clean glass;
don't be afraid of it; there's no gout in it,
and, even if there is, upon my soul it is worth
risking an attack for."

Norman Slade, a dark, wiry little man,
whose age defied all conjecture, filled his
glass gravely, and, as he tasted it, said:
"Yes, it's rare good stuff, but *you* ought to
have laid the foundation of podagra pretty
substantially by this time."

"Yes, it was the Exhibition year, and

they wanted some cavalry just to show off
before the big swells who came over to see
Paxton's glass-house," continued the Major.
"So they brigaded five regiments of light
cavalry at Hounslow, and, you may guess,
with all that going on in London, that the
way us young ones streamed up to town
every day was a caution. Except the unhappy subaltern for the day, I should think
there wasn't an officer left in any one of the
regiments."

"And you were the fellows the rest of us
were paying taxes to provide for."

"Of course you were," retorted the Major.
"We looked well, were full of go, and did
very well for ornamental purposes, which
was all you wanted in those days. We
didn't do so badly either in the Crimea as
long as we lasted; the worst of it was we
were so soon used up. However, they don't
stand those sort of larks now; do they,
Bertie?"

"Well," replied the young man addressed,

"I don't think the authorities would stand some of the things you've been recounting."

Bertie Slade was nephew to both these gentlemen. Norman's brother had married a Miss Braddock, and hence the connection; and, different as the two men were, was, strange to say, an equal favourite with both of them. No greater contrast than the two brothers-in-law could be conceived. The one, open-hearted, full of jest and story, with the art of dining as the main pursuit of his life. The other, a quiet, self-contained, reticent man, whose passion was the Turf, with a dry caustic wit of his own, who often dribbled out a thing that brought down the laugh of the smoking-room of the club to which he was affiliated. Capable, too, of biting sarcasm, if exasperated, and it was not very difficult to move Norman Slade's wrath.

"Have a glass of claret," said the Major, "or a glass of Madeira if you prefer it, while I relate another reminiscence of those times. As I have said, we all trooped up to London pretty well every day. Well, in those days there was a very famous supper-house just off the Haymarket, which was much frequented by the soldiers. Indeed, if Her Majesty's officers, to speak meta-phorically, ever did rally round the old flag, it was that particular supper-house in '51. The precious institution has long since dis-appeared, but, about three in the morning in those days, you were sure to find fellows from Woolwich, men from Hounslow, all anxious to pick up some one to share a hansom home. Indeed, as far as the Hounslow division, as they called us, went, we formed a perfect procession of hansoms; constantly ten or a dozen of them proceeding in file past Hyde Park Corner on their way to our quarters. Well, there was usually considerable difference about the fare when we arrived at Hounslow. The cabbies in-variably argued that they had waited a good bit for us, and then demanded an excessive

tariff for the time we had employed them.
Now, remember the prize-ring was by no
means dead in England in those days, and
most of us had more or less learnt to use
our hands pretty smartly; a turn-up or two
with the cabmen became at last quite an
orthodox finish to the evening, and we
seldom came home without a fare or two
being referred to the arbitration of battle.
No need to tell you that the London cabman
is pretty wideawake, and, as our fellows invariably went on the double-or-quits system,
the Hounslow lot were soon taken up by
some pretty clever bruisers amongst them.
Well, it was a bright June morning, about
five o'clock, and the cabmen were in great
feather; they had sent down that night a
couple of semi-professionals, and two or
three of our best men had been handsomely
polished off. We'd a big empty barrack-
room, containing nothing but some empty
wine-cases, where these little differences were
adjusted. They were glove-fights, you must

remember, so that our fellows didn't get so dreadfully marked as you might suppose. It was all over, the successful cabmen had carried away their double fares, and were gone, when the attention of those who were left of us was suddenly called to Jerry Moclere. I and one or two others recollected seeing him at the beginning of the scrimmage struggling with a small cabman in the corner, but we had all been too absorbed in the fight to take further note of his proceedings. Now he was sitting on a champagne-case mopping his brows with a cambric handkerchief, and exclaiming in maundering tones, ' Oh, dear, what a time I've had of it! Do, for goodness sake, get me a hammer and a few nails, some of you fellows.' ' What's the matter, Jerry ?' we exclaimed; ' what's the matter, old man ?' ' Oh, dear, what an evening I've had,' he replied, in half-crying tones. ' What a trouble he has been to me! for Heaven's sake get me a hammer and

nails. 'What do you want — what's the
matter?' we cried. 'Oh, don't,' he said,
still half-weeping; 'oh, dear, what a time
I've had. You never saw such a disagreeable little beggar.' 'What *do* you mean,
Jerry — what is it?' 'The little beast,'
he replied, in a broken voice; 'he wouldn't
go into the case, though I told him I wanted
to send him to my mother. It'll please the
dear old lady. But I've got him in at last,
thank goodness; do help me to nail him
down at once, the discontented little brute!
I can feel him still wriggling about.' 'Do
you mean to say,' we cried, 'that you've got
a man in the case?' 'Got him in?' he returned, lugubriously, 'yes, and it has taken
me the whole night to get him there. Now
do, like good fellows, bring the nails and a
direction card.' But here we thought it was
high time to intervene. Jerry, who had
attained a high state of maudlin drunken-
ness, was carried off to bed, earnestly requesting that the case might be sent by the

first train in the morning to his mother.
Of course, we deuced soon had the top off
the case, and high time, for the small cabman inside was quite past making any
further efforts on his own account. Indeed,
it required the help of a doctor to bring him
round, and a handsome solatium on Jerry's
part to hush up the business. Poor Jerry! A
shell at Balaklava, as I dare say some of you
know, killed as good a fellow as ever crossed
saddle Now, gentlemen, come along, and
we'll have a cigar and coffee downstairs."

"Well, Bertie, how's the regiment getting
on ? Still in it's chronic state of difficulties
as regards ways and means, I suppose ? "

"Yes," replied Gilbert Slade, laughing ;
" we still hold a ten-pound note in much
veneration, but, fortunately, we are not tried
quite so high at Aldershot as they were in
the days of your Hounslow campaign. The
powers that be don't stand such incessant
running up to town—a restriction which,
though unpleasant, keeps us afloat."

Gilbert Slade was a subaltern in his uncle's old corps, and, of course, amongst the seniors were several who had been in the regiment with him. Besides, the Major never missed the annual dinner, and, indeed, had much to say to its management. They said at the Albion that Major Braddock was a very fastidious gentleman, but, as the *chef* added enthusiastically, "he is a judge, and it's quite a pleasure to cook for him." So that, one way and another, Major Braddock had never lost touch of his old regiment, and knew something about pretty well every officer in it.

"I suppose you'll be moving in the spring," he said, as he lit a big cigar.

"Yes," replied Gilbert; "it's our turn to move, and, I suppose, in April we shall go to the Northern district; but where I don't exactly know—Manchester, I'm afraid."

"And why afraid?" rejoined Major Braddock. "Merchant princes, bless you, who know how the thing should be done. If

you play your cards properly, you ought to
manage to get your legs under the maho-
gany of all the best houses, and wind up
by marrying a hundred thousand pounds.
Don't tell me, sir! It's not often a young
fellow gets such a chance so early in life.
I can only say I regard it as sending the
regiment to play by the waters of Pactolus,
and it'll be a disgrace to the lot of you if
you ever know want afterwards."

"All I know is that Manchester is not a
popular quarter with the Dragoons generally," rejoined Gilbert, laughing. "However, it is by no means settled yet that that
is our destination."

"Going on leave?" asked the Major,
dryly.

"Yes—am on leave, indeed, now, though
I shall probably run back to Aldershot for a
night to arrange one or two little matters
that I left unsettled when I came away.
Then I'm going to stay for a little while
with some friends in Nottinghamshire,

where I am promised a few days with the Belvoir."

."Ah!" said the Major, "you'll have to look lively to hold your own with the Duke's. It's a rare country, and, if you've the luck to throw in for good sport, you will find it will try the best horse in your stable to live with them."

And then the conversation became general, reverting to, amongst other things—as it was apt to do in those days, what a friend of mine used to call the great annual problem, namely, what was to win the forthcoming Derby, and about this there was, needless to say, much diversity of opinion. In these days men trouble their heads very much less concerning the solving of that riddle, and it is not until the race is near at hand that much interest is manifested about it.

Gilbert Slade was a shrewd observer, and he noticed that, whereas the Major and the other men had much to say about it, and

expressed their opinions freely, pooh-pooh-
ing each other's judgment with much dis-
dain, Norman Slade, who, as Gilbert well
knew, had far more knowledge of the subject than all the others put together, smoked
silently, and listened to all the talk with a
somewhat derisive smile on his countenance.
At last he was appealed to point-blank to
give them his views on the subject.

" Can't, my good fellow," replied Norman,
drily ; " I haven't got any views about it
whatever. I simply say I don't know. If
you consider my advice worth anything, it
is merely that it is best let alone for the
present."

" Well, Norman," said the Major, laughing, " we certainly can't be said to have got
much out of you."

Slade simply shrugged his shoulders in
reply, and turned the conversation. Those
who knew Norman Slade were quite aware
of two things : first, that you might as well
try to extract information from an oyster

about any coming turf event as from him;
secondly, on the rare occasions when he
did vouchsafe a hint, it was sure to be well
worth following. Perhaps Gilbert had
been benefited as much as any man from
such hints; he was a great favourite with
that somewhat sarcastic uncle of his, and
he had the good sense never to trouble
him with questions about these matters.
Gilbert Slade had a very shrewd head on
his shoulders. He was a popular man in
his regiment, but there was a touch of his
uncle Norman's reticence about his character. He most assuredly did not wear
his heart upon his sleeve, nor did he un-
bosom himself quite so readily to his chums
as many men of his age do. So far, his
life at present could not be said to have
been eventful; he had knocked about with
his regiment from one garrison-town to
another for the last four years, had always
plenty of houses open to him in the leave-

season, and enjoyed a run in London as much as most men.

"Curious," muttered Gilbert, as he strolled homewards, "the difference between these two uncles of mine. As far as giving me a dinner goes, or writing me a moderate cheque if I got into difficulties, I've no doubt the Major would stand to me like a man; but in a serious scrape I fancy Uncle Norman would be worth a dozen of him. Every one who knows him seems to think he might have done anything if he had taken the trouble to try, while as for the Major my impression is that it is well for him his father left him very comfortably off. From all accounts he was a rattling good fellow, but a precious bad officer in the days of his soldiering. Ah! well, fortunately, I need trouble neither of them for assistance." And then Gilbert began lazily to reflect on his coming visit to Nottinghamshire, and speculate upon how much fun he could get out of the couple of hunters that he was taking down with him. When he got back to Limmer's he strolled into the coffee-room. It was tolerably late by this time, for the smoking-conclave at the Thermopolium had been of some duration, and it had been late when they had sat down to dinner.

There were some half-dozen young fellows in the coffee-room, solacing themselves as " young gentlemen laden with care" are wont to do, according to the famous lyric.

" Thought I was in for a real row to-night, coming out of Bob Croft's," said one. " They were a queer lot who rushed two fellows in front of me; but, by Jove! they caught a brace of Tartars. I never saw men hit out straighter or cleaner; and as for the leader of the gang he went down at once from a left-hander I should have been sorry to have caught, and his pals got thoroughly sick of the job in less than two minutes."

" What the deuce are you boring us with

the account of a night-house row for?
We've all seen it, and shall, doubtless, see
it again before we've done. Bertie Slade,
by Jove! What are you doing here?"

"Well, just now," said Gilbert, as he
raised his hat, smiling, "I was listening
to your friend's account of the row which
he witnessed in the Haymarket."

"Oh! there's nothing much in it, I dare
say," replied the narrator, somewhat sulkily.
"But Barton interfered, as he invariably
does, just before I came to the point of
the story. I never heard such a fearful
malediction as that man hurled after the
fellow who had struck him down, when he
picked himself up. I can't get the pale,
blood-stained face out of my head. He
evidently knew him, for he cursed him by
name, and swore never to forget nor for-
give him; vowed that his turn would come,
and that then Ralph Furzedon might look
to himself. Never heard the name before,
and don't suppose any of you did."

The company shook their heads in igno-
rance, and Gilbert, who, at all events,
considered care sufficiently dissipated for
that evening, nodded " Good-night."

CHAPTER III.

THROWN OUT.

MR. FURZEDON was a gentleman wise far beyond his years. What his antecedents were previous to his arrival at the University was a fact concerning which no one knew anything. He never alluded in the faintest way to his family. He seemed plentifully supplied with money, had avowedly not the slightest intention of taking a degree, and conformed to the rules of his college just sufficiently to prevent coming into serious collision with the authorities. He spent his money freely, but invariably with an object in view. However off-hand his invitations might seem, they were not so in reality;

and never was a young man less given to spontaneous outbursts of that description. He was by no means proud of his progenitor, though he admitted the old gentleman had behaved excessively well in quitting this world when he, Ralph, was about sixteen years old, and leaving him very comfortably off. He had come up to the University with the object solely of forming a circle of acquaintance. The men he was civil to were all such as he thought would prove useful to him in life. His father had acquired his riches by the simple process of money-lending, but Ralph Furzedon had no idea of continuing that business, profitable though it was. His ambition was to take a good social position, and college was to him a mere stepping-stone to that end. He was fairly popular, he went in for most of the games and diversions so much esteemed by the undergraduates, and, if he did not distinguish himself in any particular pursuit, still he was passably good at many things;

not, perhaps, a very amiable character, if
you knew him thoroughly, but he was much
too clever to let the spots on the sun be
seen. Young men are not usually suspicious, and very few of his companions had
the slightest idea of the ingrained selfishness
of the man's nature. It never occurred to
them that the first view that anything presented to his mind was how it would affect
him, Ralph Furzedon.

Charlie Devereux was a very popular man,
and it suited Mr. Furzedon to become intimate with him on that account; then, again,
young Devereux was an undoubtedly fine
horseman. Mr. Furzedon, in his far-sighted
sagacity, opined that in a few years Charlie
might have blossomed into a crack gentleman rider. Furzedon was very fond of a
small racing speculation, when, to use his
own language, he saw his way, and he
thought that his friend might turn out useful to him in this latter capacity later on.
Furzedon had come up to the University

late ; he had begun life for himself at the age of eighteen, and it was only after knocking about London for a couple of years that he realised how very difficult it was for a young fellow to form eligible acquaintances. Friends, as they would term themselves, were easy enough to make by a young gentleman with a liberal command of money, but, shrewd beyond his years, Ralph Furzedon was not to be imposed upon by these Brummagem imitations. He aspired to mix with gentlemen, and he knew that the very best of the acquaintance he had made had only a doubtful status in that way. For instance, he saw no possibility of getting into a decent club, and that was a point that troubled him much. It showed something for the determination of the man's character that, when he thoroughly awoke to this state of things, he made up his mind to submit to the restraints of the University, solely to attain the end he had in view. Mr. Furzedon did not intend to honour the

University much longer, but so far was very well satisfied at the results of his experiment.

Furzedon and Charlie Devereux duly carried out their programme, and arrived at North Leach. Once settled in their quarters and they lost no time in commencing the serious business of life; that is to say, hunting at every available opportunity. Charlie had come down rather late for breakfast one morning. He was a terrible sinner in that respect, and generally "stumped up" a cover-hack in the course of the season.

" We can't wait for you, Charlie," said Lettice. " Remember we're riding our hunters, whilst you no doubt have sent on, and intend riding, that luckless slave of yours."

" All right ! " rejoined Charlie, " you and Furzedon had better jog on. I shall overtake you before you get to Harroh Wood, I dare say."

Charlie, perhaps, lingered rather longer

over his breakfast than he dreamt of ; but certain it is when he turned off through a line of gates that led down to the wood he had seen nothing of Furzedon or his sister on-his way. He looked at his watch and saw that he was late ; still he fancied that the hounds had not yet left the cover. He galloped rapidly on, and, as he came to the next field, caught sight of a lady in difficulties at the gate on the far side. It had swung to, and her horse was too fidgety to allow her to open it. Again and again did she get it a little way open, and then her hunter, in his impatience to get on, twitched it out of her hand.

"Pray allow me to do that for you," exclaimed Charlie, as he raised his hat.

"Oh! thank you so much," rejoined the fair horsewoman. "Dandy is always troublesome at gates, but this morning he is behaving shamefully. You see he knows we are late, and is so dreadfully anxious about it."

By this time Charlie had got the gate open, and held it while his new acquaintance made her way through.

"I was so late," she said, gaily, as they cantered across the next field together, "that my husband declined to wait any longer for me. Husbands are capable of such things at times, and I dare say you will give the verdict against me on an occasion of this sort. But surely," she exclaimed, "we are not riding for the next gate."

"No," answered Charlie. "But I know every yard of this country by heart. If we slip through the gap at the top here, it is nothing of a jump; we shall find a similar place in the next fence, which will take us down to the top end of the cover. It's a great cut, and, if I know anything about it, we haven't a minute to spare. Listen!" he exclaimed, as the full-throated chorus rang musically on their ears. "Those hounds will be away almost immediately, if they are not already." And Charlie pressed his hack to a gallop, and led the way at a pretty sharp pace in the direction he indicated.

As they cleared the fence there was a crash of canine tongues that was a revelation to a fox-hunter.

" They are away, by Jove!" cried Charlie, " and on the far side the cover, I am afraid. I will do my best for you, but they will take a deal of catching. As for me, I am clean out of it, unless by miraculous luck I happen to pick up my hunter at the cover-side. I've rather taken it out of my hack already, and, though good of his kind, he is hardly equal to catching hounds that have slipped one."

" Too true," exclaimed the lady, as they jumped into the field adjoining the cover; " they're gone, and apparently everybody else."

Charlie made no reply, but sat down and bustled his hack round the top of the cover, his fair companion keeping close at his heels; but when he got to the other side,

and found nothing but a small group com-
posed of a couple of gamekeepers in velvet-
cens and half a-dozen labourers, he realised
that his prediction was only too fatally ful-
filled. There was no sign of his hunter,
and, worse still, no likelihood of his reaching
the hounds. These, indeed, were already
out of sight, and their vicinity only to be
judged by sundry red and black coats that
bobbed over the fences from time to time.
With difficulty Charlie suppressed a malediction on his own indolence, and then,
glancing at his companion, wondered what
view she would take of it.

"Ah!" she said, half laughing, half
pouting, "we are companions in misfor-
tune. It is aggravating to have lost a
good gallop, and still more aggravating to
know that we have only ourselves to blame
for it. Yes," she continued, as laughter
triumphed over petulance in her mood, "we
are both victims of our own Sybaritism.
We couldn't tear ourselves from our pillows

this autumn morning, nor restrain our appetites at the breakfast-table. What are we to do ?"

Charlie made no reply for some few minutes. "Lost a run," he thought, "missed my hunter, and have got a strange demoiselle thrown on my hands, whom I have no idea what to do with."

"Catching them," he answered, at last, "is out of the question. I can only suggest we follow leisurely on, and trust to the chapter of accidents to fall in with them towards the afternoon."

"Very good!" replied the lady; "and, if you will kindly accept the charge, I will place myself in your hands."

They jogged along for some little time in silence, and were now plodding along a road which, as Charlie informed his companion, would bring them to Narcham Gorse, a cover which, he continued to explain, it was very probable that the fox would make for. But on arriving at that

favourite refuge of foxes they found no
signs of the hunt; in short, they had now
utterly lost the hounds, and were like people
adrift in the desert, as far as having any
recognised point to aim for. All inquiries
proved useless; none of the farmers or
labourers whom Charlie questioned had seen
"aught of the hounds" that day. As for the
lady, she bore her disappointment with great
equanimity, and even laughed at the *fiasco*.

"I don't know whether you keep a hunting diary," she said, at length. "I do:
but I don't think I shall make any entries
concerning this day."

"Well, I don't," replied Charlie; "if I
did I should simply write down, 'Was an
indolent idiot.' I've no doubt it has been
the run of the season, so far. What a fool
I shall feel when they are all talking it
over at dinner this evening!"

"You won't deem me too curious," said
his fair companion, "if I ask the name of
my fellow-sufferer?"

"I am Charles Devereux," he replied, "and live at North Leach, where we have been settled time out of mind."

"Devereux!" she replied. "You are a brother, no doubt, of that handsome Miss Devereux who rides so well; we are neighbours; my husband, Major Kynaston, has taken The Firs, as no doubt you know, for the season."

"Yes," replied Charlie, "I know the place very well. It is about ten miles from us. I hope you like it. The owner never lives in it, but it is nearly always let for the hunting season, though people don't so much care about it in the summer time. The fact is, it is a widely-scattered neighbourhood, and, though we natives don't mind the long distances between our houses, yet strangers are apt to think them impossible."

"They certainly strike me in that wise," replied Mrs. Kynaston laughing, "though I suppose, after all, it doesn't matter if you

have plenty of horses. But, if I mistake
not, I turn off here, and so shall no longer
be a trouble to you ?"

"Yes, you are close at home, which I
only wish I was. My horse will have had
enough of it before I get him back."

"Good-bye," replied Mrs. Kynaston, as
she extended her hand; "I trust the next
time we meet it will be not to pass such
an unprofitable day."

Mrs. Kynaston laughed as she trotted
homewards. "It is a blow, a sad blow, my
dear," she muttered to herself; "your good-
looking cavalier was blind, both to your
charms and his opportunities. There are
plenty of men I wot of who would have
thought a day well spent at Kate Kynaston's bridle-rein. This fox-hunting is a
very brutalising amusement. I don't believe Mr. Devereux knows what I'm like
this minute. He was chafing all the way
at having lost his beloved sport. As a gentleman, he couldn't refuse to take care of

an errant waif like myself; but I really believe if he had come across the hounds I should have been left to follow him as I best might. It is fortunate I had nothing to do with his mishap, or I veritably believe he would never have spoken to me again."

Mrs. Kynaston had read young Devereux pretty accurately. Charlie was bitterly disappointed at his misadventure. That young gentleman, although by no means insensible to his fair companion's charms, was an enthusiast about hunting. As before said, he rode well, and at twenty-one it was excusable that he should be a little conceited about it ; no woman's smile at present could compare in his eyes with having had all the best of a real good fifty minutes, and now, after having missed all his fun, here he was with a good many weary miles to jog home on a tired horse, and haunted with the idea that there had been a real good run. And he had good grounds for so

thinking. He knew that they had found
and slipped away, certainly at a rare pace
to start with, as he knew from the glimpse
he had got of what might be termed the tail
of the field. The hounds and the leading
division he had never caught sight of.
Then he wondered how Furzedon had got on.
Then came speculation as to what luck had
attended his chief rivals. Had they been
lucky in getting away ? Whom had fortune
favoured ? And who could lay claim to the
proud distinction of having been in front
throughout ? Then he began to think once
more of his late companion. " Yes," he
reflected critically, " she is a pretty woman,
and sits her horse very nicely. She was got
up, too, most correctly. I wonder whether
she is much of a horsewoman, and what sort
of a fellow Major Kynaston is. Keen, I
should say, or he wouldn't have left his wife
to follow on by herself. I don't suppose my
people know them yet, or I should have
heard Lettice speak of them. Hold up, old

man!" he exclaimed, as his hack made an
awkward stumble, " we've only another four
miles to do now, and you shall take your
own time to do it, only don't go to sleep
over it." The hack seemed to understand
what his master said to him, for he pricked
up his ears and proceeded of his own accord
to jog on. It was probable that he awoke to
the fact that he was pretty close to his own
stable, and determined that the sooner he
got his day's work over the better. Charlie,
as he anticipated, found himself the first
home, as he had been the last to start.
That he should vent his ill-humour on the
luckless groom who had charge of the miss-
ing hunter was only natural. The poor
fellow had done his best, but, his master not
turning up, he had had to act on his own
inspiration, and had unfortunately waited at
the wrong end of the cover. He had then
followed at a respectful distance, with three
or four second horsemen who had fallen into
the same mistake. This much only could

he tell—that the hounds had run straight
away from him, and this by no means
assuaged the wrath of his angry master,
who, having informed him that he was a
perfect idiot, strode into the house. As the
groom remarked to his fellows, with considerable justice, "It wasn't my fault. How
am I to know which end of a wood a fox
will break? If Mr. Charles had only been
in time we should have changed horses all
right, and then he could have judged for
hisself."

Mr. Charles Devereux that night at dinner
found that his instinct had not deceived
him. He had to face a fire of merciless
chaff about his coffee-housing proclivities.
He learnt that they had had a capital run
with their first fox, who, after an hour and
forty minutes, with only one check, had
fairly beaten them; how that they had a
capital second gallop in the afternoon after
a fox which was brought satisfactorily to
hand; and then, after the manner of sports-

men over their wine, they spared never a
point nor detail of the day's doings. They
quoted every village and cover they had
been near; from Winnington Scrubs to
Bubbleton Brook, not a point was spared
him; till even Furzedon, who had gone
satisfactorily to himself through the whole
business, rather winced under this little
geographical victory. Especially cruel to
the outsiders are fox-hunters when they get
to full cry over the wine-cup, and recount
their wondrous exploits over Dabchick Pas-
tures, or some similar locality, in which
nobody but a fox-hunter or a parish doctor
ever found themselves; and then came a
sharp cross-examination of how Charlie himself had spent his day; but his answers were
so curt and sulky, and his ill-humour concerning his mishap so very palpable, that
they very soon gave over teazing him. One
thing was curious—that the name of Mrs.
Kynaston never passed his lips; whether it
was accident, or whether he thought the

admission would lead to further banter on the part of his sister and Furzedon, I can't say; there merely remains the fact that it was so.

CHAPTER IV.

"LINCOLN SPRING."

LINCOLN RACES! The budding of the Turf
campaign, the first burst of spring for that
mysterious world which regulates its winter
by the Racing Calendar without respect to
weather or almanac; a meeting sometimes
postponed from frost and snow, but run off
as a rule in bitter weather, and yet which
attracts to it all the sport-loving denizens of
the adjoining counties, to say nothing of
that great body to whom racing is a business, and who have been growling over the
inaction of the last two or three months.
There is money to be made at Lincoln, no
doubt, though it more often falls to the

bookmaker to gather it than to the sanguine
backer who so boldly invests his capital on
some probably half-trained horse, of whose
present form the stable have but a misty
idea.   But, besides these, there are the great
hunting contingents from Yorkshire, from
Nottinghamshire, and Leicestershire.   Hard
riders from the Quorn, the Pytchley, and
the Bedale, from the Fitzwilliam, from the
Brocklesby, and the Belvoir—all interested
in the Open Steeplechase, the Hunt, and
the Gone Away Plate, for any of which it
is probable that some of these, or, for the
matter of that, half-a-dozen other well-
known packs, may have sent a competitor.

On a drag, opposite the Grand Stand,
were congregated most of the people mentioned in the previous chapter.   North
Leach had come down a strong party to
the races.   Old Tom Devereux and all his
family were there, and with them were the
Kynastons, for by this time a considerable
intimacy had sprung up between the two

houses; and then, had not both Tom Devereux and Major Kynaston got a horse
running? The old man was as keen as
possible to see his son ride the winner, both
of the Hunt Steeplechase and the Gone
Away Plate. In the former the Devereuxes
had entered their four-year-old, of which
Miss Lettice had thought so highly at the
beginning of the hunting-season, while the
Major had picked up something a little
before Christmas, that he had ascertained
was pretty fast, and had hunted it just
sufficiently to qualify. The North Leach
people, indeed, knew very little about the
Major's mysterious purchase. Seen him,
of course, they had; but, whether Mrs.
Kynaston was on his back or the Major, he
was never seen prominently, if there was
anything like a run. The lady, although
she rode nicely, was by no means given to
hard riding. She enjoyed the sport in her
own way, and by no means aspired to
eclipse others of her sex that might be

out, by witching horsemanship. Charlie
Devereux was by this time amongst Mrs.
Kynaston's devoted admirers, and she had
not a few. One special trait that recom-
mended her much in that young gentleman's eyes was that she did not want a
" lead," or expect to be taken care of after
the find, and always bade him not waste his
chance of a good start by dallying too long
at her side. About the Major nobody in
that country knew much, although there
were plenty of people in the London world
that could have told a good deal concerning
him.

Lounging on the lawn, his hands buried
in the pockets of his ulster, was Gilbert
Slade; he had come across with some friends
from the country-house in which he was
staying to see the first big handicap of the
season run, and at this moment one of his
friends came up, and suggested that they
should go up to the top of the stand and see
the race. Gilbert readily assented.

" It's a grind to get there," he said, " but
there's nowhere that you can see the race so
well from;" and the two accordingly toiled
up the narrow little stone staircase that led
to the roof, which they found already thickly
peopled.

"How are you, Jocelyn?" said a tall,
good-looking fellow, standing a pace or two
in advance of them. " Bitter cold weather,
isn't it? Have you got a wager on this
affair?"

" No," replied the other, " it isn't often I
indulge in that wise."

" Nor I," was the reply; " if I ever did,
I should have been tempted this time; the
joint owners of the Siren are wonderfully
confident, and have insisted on all our
leading people about here backing their
jacket."

" It is too late now," said Gilbert, " or
else I would have had a trifle on that tip."

The horses were already mustering under
the starter's hand. Two or three false starts,

and then they get off on moderately level terms.

"Well, the owners of the Siren should be satisfied," exclaimed the tall young fellow who had before addressed them. "The only thing they were afraid of was their mare getting a bad start, but she's got off right in front."

For once the owners of the hot favourite had proved right in their calculations concerning a big handicap; before they had gone a quarter of a mile the Siren had got a clean lead of her field, and from that out, she never caused her backers one moment's uneasiness. She went on improving her lead, was never even approached, and finally ran home an easy winner by half-a-dozen lengths.

"Well," said Gilbert, "I never saw such a procession as that in my life in a big race; and, now it is over, I vote we forage for food. A north-east wind makes one confoundedly hungry."

"Ah! I'm afraid you'll have to rough it rather in that respect. There is not that magnificent choice of luncheon that generally presents itself at Ascot."

They made their way slowly down the crowded staircase, and went into the luncheon-room, but it was thronged; and there was apparently small chance of obtaining even standing room at one of the tables.

"Ah!" said Jocelyn, laughing, "you will have to control your unholy appetite for some time longer. When we do get an opening, it will be useless; these locusts will have devoured everything."

"Let's come away," rejoined Gilbert with a smile. "It's too much for a man in my state to watch his fellow-creatures feed." And the two young men pushed their way downstairs with the determination of assuaging their hunger with tobacco.

They had barely reached the centre of the lawn, when a portly clean-shaven gentle-

man, with rosy cheeks and a good-humoured
smile on his face, suddenly exclaimed,
" Good-day, Mr. Jocelyn, I hope you like
the chestnut ? "

" Best horse I've got in my stable, Devereux. I only wish I could afford to come to
you for another. You never miss Lincoln
Spring, do you ? "

" No, nor the Autumn either; but we've
come down a large party this time. We're
going to have a shy at a couple of the local
races. There's a coach-load of us all come
to see Charlie win, we hope. By the way,
gentlemen, will you have a glass of champagne ? or mebbe you've had no lunch; I
know by old experience that it's pretty
rough-and-tumble work getting anything to
eat in there."

" Well, we couldn't, Devereux, and that's
all about it," replied Jocelyn laughing; "if
you can give us anything, you'd be doing
a real charity."

" Come along," said the old gentleman,

with a jolly laugh. "The missus, when she has an outing, likes to do it comfortable, and you may depend upon it, when she gets on the coach it's well victualled."

"Manna in the wilderness, by Jove," whispered Gilbert as they followed the old gentleman across to his drag, where the *débris* of luncheon still lingered.

The two gentlemen were quickly introduced to the ladies, and hospitable Mrs. Devereux insisted upon their coming up on the drag, and having their luncheon " quite comfortable."

" I think we have met before, Mr. Slade," said Mrs. Kynaston, with a bright smile.

"Of course," replied Gilbert, " I remember you at Lady Ramsbury's garden-party."

"Ah, Mr. Slade," said the lady laughing, " I'll give you one bit of advice. There is nothing so dangerous as remembering too much. It couldn't have been at Lady Ramsbury's, because I don't know her, but I came down to one of the big Aldershot

field-days last summer, and you lunched us
all in your mess-room before we returned to
town. The care Mr. Slade took of me on
that occasion made a deeper impression on
me than my charms did upon him."

"To be sure; very stupid of me," rejoined Gilbert, coolly, "that's the worst of a
London season : one does get places mud-
dled up so."

"Ah, you'll remember me another time.
I'm about to embalm myself in your memory. Let me give you some of this pigeon-
pie, and next time we meet you'll murmur
to yourself, 'She fed me when I was
hungry.'"

"Thank you," rejoined Gilbert, laughing,
"and if you could only guess how hungry I
am, Mrs. Devereux. I am perfectly ashamed
of my appetite."

"Can't pay me a better compliment," rejoined that lady. "I know, then, my cook
has done her duty."

Neither Jocelyn nor Gilbert Slade were in

any hurry to quit their new quarters. They could see there just as well as from the Grand Stand; while, as for the ladies, swathed in furs and rugs, there was no temptation for them to leave their seats. Old Tom Devereux was backwards and forwards between the drag and the betting-lawn continuously. He had a large and numerous acquaintance, and was constantly shaking hands and exchanging jokes with old friends. Suddenly Gilbert's attention was diverted from the lively conversation he was holding with Mrs. Kynaston by an exclamation from Miss Devereux.

"Good gracious! Mr. Furzedon," she cried; " I never dreamt of seeing you here."

" Ah ! I was bound to come down," he replied, " to see how the horse that carried you so well last winter acquits himself in the Hunt Steeplechase ; and, from the hint I got in town a day or two ago, I thought I might find it profitable to get here in time for the big handicap."

" And I hope it has proved so," said Miss Devereux.

" Yes, thank you," he replied; " I had a very good race. No, nothing, thank you, Mrs. Devereux; I did all that at the Great Northern, before I came up to the course."

" Furzedon," thought Gilbert, " where was it I heard that name only the other day? Ah!" he muttered to himself, " in Limmer's Coffee Room. That's the man they mentioned as having felled an unhappy wretch in the Haymarket, who hurled after him a malediction so terrible as to have attracted the attention of those fellows who saw it, and they were a festive lot, to whom a row in those parts was no novelty;" and then Gilbert dismissed the matter from his mind, and turned once more to his fair companion.

And now the numbers went up for the Gone Away Plate, and there was great excitement on the top of the drag to see Charlie's performance. Both Mrs. Kynaston and Lettice had a small venture on the success of Charlie's mount, which they regarded as already won. Could they have overheard a conversation between the Major and a seedy, sinister individual at the back of the betting-ring, they would not have felt quite so sanguine about the result.

" Ah, Major," said the latter, " I knows your horse well. Knew him before you had him, and you're quite right ; he's just the sort to pick up these hunter's stakes on the flat ; but, I warn you, you haven't got it all your own way this time. There's another party trying just the same game. I've no idea which of you has got the best of it ; but remember there's another horse in the race which is no more a hunter than yours is "

" Your're sure of what you say, Prance? "

" Quite," rejoined the other.

" Confound it. I've got a good bit of money on this."

" Well, you tell your jockey to keep his

eye on The Decoy. And now, Major, times are hard, and I give you my word that information is worth a sovereign to you."

The Major paused for a second, and then unbuttoned his overcoat, took the coin from his waistcoat pocket, and handed it to his companion.

"Thank you, sir," replied the tout, for such he was. "I've always run straight with you, Major, and I'm quite sure of what I tell you. Yours and The Decoy will run first and second, and it'll be a race between 'em. I hope, for your sake, sir, yours is good enough to win," and thereupon Mr. Prance vanished with the utmost celerity, and immediately invested the sovereign he had just received with a ready-money bookmaker on Decoy.

Great was the excitement on the top of the drag as the competitors for the Gone Away Plate, after galloping three-quarters of the distance, turned into the straight, and the Major's black jacket was seen with a

clear lead, and a cry arose from the Stand of
" Rob Roy wins ! " " Rob Roy in a canter ! "
But Mr. Prance had been only too correct
in his diagnosis of the race.

As he came away from his field, Charlie
looked anxiously right and left for The
Decoy, as the Major at the last moment had
told him that that was the one quarter from
which he might apprehend danger. But
the gentleman on The Decoy was no neo-
phyte ; he had ridden many more races, was
far more cunning of fence than Charlie, and
quite aware that he had nothing but Rob
Roy to beat. Trusting to Charlie's inexpe-
rience, the minute he came away he followed directly in his track ; the former,
casting anxious glances right and left, could
see nothing of his dangerous adversary, and,
though somewhat astonished at the non-
appearance of The Decoy, Charlie raced
steadily home. Suddenly, just before reaching the Stand, like a flash, he saw the white
jacket and crimson belt of Mr. Sexton's

mare at his girths.   It flurried him a little,
no doubt, as the being caught close to home
does most men in their first public race;
still, he kept his head fairly well, and it
wasn't till he saw that his opponent had
more than collared him opposite to the
Stand that he sat down and began riding
in earnest.   But it was no use, his crafty
opponent had already got a neck the best
of him, and, to say nothing of being on,
perhaps, the better horse, was certainly the
more experienced " finisher " of the pair.
He, too, began to ride his horse in resolute
fashion, and not only held the advantage
he had gained, but improved it to a good
half-length before he passed the winning-
post.

There was wailing, half earnest and half
laughing, on the top of the drag at the
defeat of their champion.   There were bitter
maledictions on the part of the Major as to
what he was pleased to term Mr. Sexton's
unscrupulous conduct, totally ignoring that

Mr. Sexton had only succeeded, and that he had failed; that otherwise their proceedings had been precisely similar; and there was considerable hilarity on the part of Mr. Prance, who had succeeded in adding three sovereigns to his store.

" Very bad, Miss Devereux," said Slade; " but we can only say that your brother, though defeated, was not disgraced. No man could have made a better struggle for it, and we can only say that it was his ill-luck to encounter an enemy a little too good for him."

I doubt whether Gilbert's uncle, Norman, would have given quite so merciful a verdict. I think he would have said, " He rides very nicely for a young one, but the old practitioner did him at the finish. If he had made the most of the commanding position he held when he got into the straight, I should doubt The Decoy ever having caught him."

" Good-bye, Mrs. Devereux," said Slade.

"Of course we shall see you all here to-morrow, and then I trust your own jacket will be hailed the winner. In the meantime, Miss Devereux, let me thank you for your kindness to a couple of famishing wayfarers. And now here come your horses, and we must say good-bye."

"Good-bye," returned the hospitable old lady. "Good-bye, Mr. Jocelyn. Remember, I shall expect you both to luncheon to-morrow."

And, with a cordial adieu all round, the two young men took their departure.

"Deuced good find that," said Gilbert, as he and Jocelyn walked back to Lincoln. "Very pleasant people, and they have entertained us royally. What are they exactly?"

"People who have farmed in the Wolds for centuries, and on a large scale. The old man is held in the highest respect, and almost treated as a squire by the scattered gentlemen around him. As for Mrs. Kynaston, you apparently know more about her than I do. I hope they'll pull off the Hunt Steeplechase to-morrow, for they were evidently sadly disappointed about being beaten to-day."

CHAPTER V.

THE HUNT STEEPLECHASE.

THE next day was a great improvement on its predecessor: the wind was still keen, but there was very little of it, and a bright sun not only threw out considerable heat, but also had an enlivening effect on people's spirits. Mr. Prance, in high feather at his yesterday's success over the Gone Away Plate, was, for a gentleman of his saturnine temperament, quite genial, and was laughing and jesting with two or three of his mates — racecourse hangers-on—who, like himself, picked up a precarious living in a by no means strait-laced fashion. Suddenly the man's manner was utterly transformed; he started as if he had been stung; and, had any of those who had witnessed the *fracas* in the Haymarket been present to see, they would have noticed the same look of implacable resentment which had so arrested their attention on that evening. The cause was not far to seek, for they had just passed Mr. Furzedon strolling leisurely up the course with a friend.

"Ah!" muttered Mr. Prance to himself, "let me ever have the chance, and if I don't give you quittance in full, Mr. Furzedon, for all I owe you, may my hand and tongue be numb for ever in this world!"

Mr. Furzedon, quite unconscious of the very questionable blessing invoked on his head, passed on. It is doubtful whether he would have been much perturbed at Mr. Prance's thirst for vengeance had he been aware of it. He was far too conscious of his superior physical strength, to say nothing of his infinitely superior position, to feel any anxiety about any harm such a man as Prance could work him. That the cause of quarrel between the two lay deeper than the blow he had struck him that night outside the supper-rooms had been transparent even to the casual spectators, but what that was must at present remain a matter between themselves. One of the first persons the tout came across when he had made his way into the inclosure was Major Kynaston, who was carefully studying his race-card.

"Well, sir," he said, "what I told you yesterday was right enough; and it was a very close fit between yours and The Decoy."

"Yes, you were right enough, my man; and, change the jockeys, and it is possible it might have been the other way. Not but what Mr. Devereux rode very nicely; still the old hand, of course, proved a little too much for the young one. Race-riding, like everything else, requires a lot of practice; it was pretty well my man's first

appearance in public, while Mr. Long has
been riding for years. However, your
information was worth the sovereign."

"Thank you, sir," replied Prance; "if I
find out anything to-day I'll let you know."

The Major nodded; he could take pretty
good care of himself on a racecourse, and
was by no means to be led away by what
he might pick up from a tout; Prance, he
knew from former experience, was worth
listening to, and now and again, as in the
case of yesterday's race, really had come by
a bit of genuine information.

Tom Devereux's drag, it need scarcely be
said, was early drawn up opposite the Stand.
The ladies were in high spirits, and confident in the extreme about victory to-day
in the Hunt Steeplechase. In vain Charlie
protested against such extreme confidence.
"I've a good horse, I know, Lettice," he
said; "but I may meet a better, just as I
did yesterday."

"It won't do, Charlie," replied the girl;

" we are bent upon returning victors to North Leach, and mind you don't disappoint us."

By this time the drag was surrounded by several young men, amongst whom Gilbert Slade, Jocelyn, and Furzedon were prominent.

" I suppose you are very fond of racing, Miss Devereux ?" said Gilbert Slade, who had climbed to the roof of the drag.

" Fond of it?" she replied. " I can hardly say. I know next to nothing about it. We always take the coach to Doncaster, and I have been there two or three times. My father knows Lincoln races well; but neither mother nor I ever came here before; and this time it is in honour of Charlie's first appearance as a rider at the big meeting of his county."

" Then you are ignorant of the glories of Ascot and Goodwood ?" said Slade.

" Utterly," replied Miss Devereux. " I know very little of London and its gaieties,

although, of course, I am aware what great
gatherings of fashion those two race-meet-
ings are. We are very plain, humdrum
people. A run to the sea when the crops are
in constitutes our summer gaiety, though
occasionally I get asked to my aunt's in
South Kensington. She is papa's sister,
you must know, and married a man who
was in some kind of business in London,
I'm sure I don't know what, but he has left
her a very comfortably-off widow, and she
knows a lot of people, and I always have a
very pleasant time when I go to stay with
her."

"Ah! I daresy Mrs. —— I beg your
pardon, what did you say your aunt's name
was?" said Slade.

"I didn't mention it," rejoined Lettice,
smiling, "but it is Mrs. Connop, and she
lives in Onslow Gardens. She is a very
bustling woman, who enjoys life keenly,
entertains herself a good deal, and goes to
everything. I have always had a very gay

six weeks with her, and that's all I ever
know of London dissipation. You, I dare
say, have had years and years of it?"

"I have had my fling," rejoined Slade,
quietly; "but I am a soldier, and am very
often quartered a long way from London.
Just at present I am at Aldershot; but we
expect to move northwards in a couple of
months, and, though I dare say I shall
manage a month or six weeks, it will be,
like yourself, a mere gulp at the wine-cup,
but no draining of the goblet to the dregs;
I only trust that we shall meet."

"I haven't been asked yet," rejoined Miss
Devereux, "and that is the first and most
important step in my London season! But
there, the numbers are up surely for the
next race."

"Ah!" rejoined Gilbert, laughing, "I am
afraid they have just finished that race, and
we have actually been gossiping during the
contest. Never mind, it was only a small
selling affair; and I don't suppose any of us

are really interested in anything but the Hunt Steeplechase."

"Now," said Mrs. Kynaston, with a little grimace, "there must be an end to all this idle gossip. The serious business of the day is about to commence—we have done with the *entrées*, and come to the *pièce de résistance*. I have got a fortune on the sky-blue jacket and white sleeves. I don't often go in for a gamble, but I have asked Mr. Furzedon to put me ten pounds on Pole Star."

' That's plunging with a vengeance," rejoined Lettice, "and you ought really to win a good deal of money. But Charlie tells me that he has got me fifty pounds to five about his mount."

"Yes," interrupted Jocelyn, "you're entitled to a good price, Miss Devereux. I don't suppose even your father or your brother are backing Pole Star heavily, and the Fletchers are supposed to farm this race —to enjoy almost a monopoly of it. The

only thing that ever puzzles us is which to
back of the two brothers, George or Jim;
they're about equally good horsemen, and
the difficulty is to find out which is riding
the best horse."

"And what are they doing about these
formidable brothers now?" inquired Mrs.
Kynaston.

"George Fletcher's mount is first favourite," replied Jocelyn, "but I noticed some
very shrewd farmers taking the longer odds
about Jim's horse. Don't think me a rene-
gade, Miss Devereux; I have backed your
brother, but I have also got a trifle on Jim
Fletcher."

And now the horses, having paced past
the Stand, come thundering down again in
their preliminary canter. Nothing, perhaps,
goes better than a big raking chestnut that
Charlie Devereux is handling; the favourite
looks "fit" as hands can make him, and is
pronounced a nice "mover" by the *cogno-
scenti*, and the men of the Midlands have

keen eyes for that sort of thing. There is a
varmint wear-and-tear look, too, about Jim
Fletcher's mount that led good judges to
think he might prove troublesome to the
winner at the finish. Still, although out of
the half-score runners they were all backed
more or less, yet it was quite evident that
the Ring, as well as the backers generally,
believed in nothing but the Fletchers.
George's horse Rattle, indeed, was a hot
favourite, and Jim Fletcher's mount advanced so rapidly in public estimation, that
when the starter mustered the horses it was
quoted at only a couple of points behind his
brother's. It is not very difficult to dis-
patch a lot of horses on a three-mile race.
A few lengths, which are often never to be
recovered in a short distance on the flat, are
of very little account in the long cross-
country journey, and in a very few minutes
they are away. For the first half-mile
nothing takes a very decided lead; at the
end of that time Jim Fletcher's blue jacket

shoots decidedly to the front, and many of his backers at once deplore their infatuation, as they murmur,

"The favourite's the real pea, after all, and Jim is only making running for his brother"; and that this impression was shared by the jockeys riding in the race seemed probable, as Charlie Devereux and the rest of them waited in a cluster upon George Fletcher, who was distinguished from his brother by wearing a red cap and belt.

In the meantime Jim sailed gaily away, his varmint-looking steed jumping in faultless fashion, until he had stolen a lead of nearly a field from his opponents. Half the distance had now been traversed, and, young though Charlie Devereux was at the business, it suddenly occurred to him, as it also did to one of his companions in a bright green jacket, that they were letting Jim Fletcher get a very dangerous distance in front; he turned it over for a few seconds in his mind, and the minute they had cleared

the next fence he shot to the front, closely
attended by the green jacket, and, a little to
his bewilderment, by George Fletcher. That
latter worthy laughed low in his beard as
he muttered,

"It's getting about time to give the
backers of the favourite a show for their
money; but if Jim ever lets us catch him
now he is a much bigger fool than I think
him."

Mrs. Kynaston was a lady who had seen
a good deal of racing one way and the
other, and, what is more, was really a very
fair judge when she did see it.

"I am afraid they have let the blue jacket
slip them," she said; "they have let him gain
such a tremendous lead, they'll never succeed
in catching him. However, Mr. Devereux
seems quite alive to the situation now."

Jim Fletcher continued to pursue the even
tenor of his way. Now and again he shot a
glance over his shoulder, but could see no
antagonist near him.

"They can't intend me to come in alone, surely," he thought.

But already Charlie, closely attended by George Fletcher, the green jacket, and one or two others, was rapidly diminishing the wide gap that lay between himself and the leader.

"Ah," exclaimed Miss Devereux, "they will catch the black jacket now by the time they enter the straight!"

"Yes," said Mrs. Kynaston; "my only fear is that he has been rather hard upon Pole Star in doing so, and that he will find that he has not much left in his horse just when the pinch comes."

Miss Devereux was quite right. As Jim Fletcher jumped the fence on to the race-course, his companions had begun to take close order with him, but he still held a four lengths' lead of Pole Star. But there was just this difference: whereas Jim Fletcher's horse jumped well and cleanly, Pole Star, for the first time, fenced in slovenly fashion. There was nothing now between the competitors and the winning-post but a hurdle about half-way up the straight— nothing of a jump, but just the sort of thing to bother a beaten horse. Charlie was still lying second, with the green jacket waiting at his quarters. Steadily he crept up, and as they neared the hurdle Jim Fletcher held a bare two lengths' lead. But there was this difference between him and his antagonists : he had never bustled or called upon his horse the whole way round. Zadkiel, the leader, jumps it beautifully, but Pole Star hits it heavily, and blunders nearly on his knees, and, quickly though Charlie recovers him, the *contretemps* is fatal; before he can fairly set his horse going again the green jacket has passed him, and George Fletcher is alongside of him ; but Zadkiel's rider is not the man to throw away a chance. His horse is going strong with him, and he comes right away at once. Desperately though the green jacket rides his horse he cannot get within hail of the leader, while Charlie and George Fletcher, after one brief call upon their steeds, ceased riding, and finished third and fourth respectively.

" Yes," said the Major, as he watched the race from that high bit of scaffolding, designated as the Stand, in Tattersall's Ring, " I was right — quite right. My dear young friend, till you've had a good bit more practice, it is throwing money into the fire to back your mount. You would have about won to-day if you had not been so completely humbugged by those Fletchers. I should like to know them; they've a very pretty idea of picking up a race. To win with a horse that was supposed to be making running while the field were all waiting on the favourite is ingenious. Prance was right. He said he couldn't make out which, but that one of the Fletchers would take that steeplechase for certain. I haven't done so badly over it, but, of course, I mustn't admit that; they will think it rank heresy over the way if I acknowledge to having followed anything but the Devereux colours."

"Oh, dear," cried Miss Devereux, on the box of the drag, "what a piece of bad luck! I'm sure Pole Star wouldn't have been beaten if it hadn't been for that unlucky mistake at the last hurdle."

"No," said Mrs. Kynaston, quietly, "there's a great deal of luck in racing, and this, unfortunately, wasn't run to suit your brother. Better luck next time, Lettice."

Mrs. Kynaston knew a great deal better than that. She was perfectly aware of how the race had been run, and why Pole Star had blundered so badly at the last hurdle— seen it all, indeed, just as clearly as her husband, but she was not the woman to make herself unpleasant by insinuations of that sort, and so they had another glass of champagne all round, and indulged in strong tirades against the shameful machi- nations of the Fletchers, and agreed that

tricks of this description were not legiti-
mate, and that the Fletchers ought to be
ashamed of themselves.

People who lose their money are somewhat apt to argue in this wise. There was
nothing inadmissible in the tactics of the
Fletchers. All that could be fairly said was
that their opponents, had they not been
rather inexperienced, would never have been
fooled by them, and yet practised jockeys
have fallen into similar error.

At this juncture Charlie Devereux appeared at the side of the coach. "Awful
sorry, Lettice," he said. "I apologise all
round. I really think I had a pretty good
chance, but the Fletchers gammoned me
out of the race. So sorry I lost your money,
Mrs. Kynaston, but I plead guilty to having
been green as any gosling. When I recognised the trap they had laid for us it was
too late. I had to be so hard on Pole
Star to catch Jim Fletcher that it is little
wonder my horse had had enough of it when
we got into the straight."

"Never mind, Mr. Devereux, you'll ride the winner of the Liverpool before two or three years are over. All trades require a little practice; and," she said, leaning over the coach to speak to him, "you *can* ride, you know."

Charlie made no reply, but, if ever eyes acknowledged the balm poured into wounded vanity, his did. Men, and more especially young men, are wont to think tenderly of women who bind up their hurts in this wise. Charlie concealed his feelings tolerably well, but he felt in his heart that he had thrown the race away, and firmly believed that, if he had never let Jim Fletcher get more than some ten or a dozen lengths in front of him, he would have beaten him. And now the horses come up, and, with many hand-shakes and hearty wishes for meeting again, the little party breaks up, the Devereuxes and Kynastons returning to North Leach, while Gilbert Slade and Mr. Jocelyn again crossed the Nottinghamshire border.

CHAPTER VI.

SIR RONALD RADCLIFFE.

THE bitter north-east wind has at last departed, the swallows in scores are cutting the clear, pure, sweet air. The spring handicaps are things of the past; the trees are in all the glory of their early foliage; and spring is fast melting into summer.

The London season is in full swing; strawberries are rapidly becoming within the reach of people of moderates incomes; the Derby has been lost and won, and Ascot is a thing to be looked back upon with feelings of bitter anguish, or joyous murmurs of victory. The Row is all alive this bright June morning, thronged with the votaries of fashion, thronged with those who would fain pass as such, crowded with cynics who watch the gaudy parade with scoffing eyes. Yes, with struggling young men, who only wish their profession would leave them no leisure to show there; with men who cannot get rid of their weariness; with men who have quite got rid of their money, but cling to the gay pageant from habit, and as the cheapest amusement that is left to them; young ladies, whose rosy cheeks, sparkling eyes, and animated manner betoken that they are new to the joys of the season; their more experienced sisters, with the languid air of those who have awoke to the knowledge that "the gilt is off the gingerbread"; veteran campaigners, both married and single, painfully alive to the misery of their exacting dress-makers, wearily conscious of those four new dresses for Ascot that have produced no results; the equestrians canter up and down with careless smile, as if Care never sat behind the horse-

man, although young Locksley wonders
whether his hack will ever be paid for;
while Mr. Manners carries a note in his
breast-pocket from McGillup, the livery-
stable keeper, with an intimation that that
is the last mount he can be supplied with
till he, McGillup, has had something on
account.

Looking on at the queer raree-show is a
man who seldom troubles it. A slight, wiry,
clean-shaved man, with keen dark eyes and
a most determined expression about the
mouth. He stoops slightly, and his hair is
heavily shot with grey; his dress is peculiar,
scrupulously neat, but slightly old-fashioned;
but, though Norman Slade would never have
been accused of spending much money on
his attire, yet the man would have been a
very poor judge indeed who took him for
anything but a gentleman. He has possessed himself of a chair, and, having lighted
a cigar, sits there ruminating. He seldom
has occasion to raise his hat, for with ladies

his acquaintance seems to be very limited. But with the other sex it is different. Nod after nod is exchanged with Norman, and many of those who salute him are members of the aristocracy, or well-known men about town. Norman Slade, although his name figures neither in the " Peerage " nor in Burke's " Landed Gentry," comes of a good and perfectly well-known family; but it is chiefly through his passion for the Turf and his long career about town that he has acquired the numerous acquaintances which he undoubtedly possesses. Men, as a rule, like and respect, but are just a little afraid of, Norman; he is what is termed " thoroughly straight," a word of great significance on the Turf; he is an excellent companion, full of anecdote, and can be most amusing when pleased with those about him. But, as before said, he has a rough edge to his tongue, and, if annoyed, can be bitterly sarcastic. He has lounged into the Park this morning to indulge in what he calls a " think." During the past week he has met Major Kynaston at dinner, and it is not to be supposed that, although he had never encountered him, a man like Norman Slade did not know Major Kynaston pretty well by repute. The Major enjoyed a reputation that even he would have deemed it desirable to bury if possible; nobody could have brought any direct charge against him, but it is equally certain that nobody would ever have described the Major as " thoroughly straight." He was notoriously lucky at *écarté*, and, indeed, at cards generally, while he was equally considered a terribly sharp practitioner in his betting transactions.

Of all this Norman Slade was well aware; but what was it to him? He would have grinned at the idea of the Major inveigling him into any little things to his detriment on either card-table or race-course; but at this dinner Major Kynaston had not only mentioned having made the acquaintance

of Gilbert, but had very much exaggerated
the extent of their intimacy. Now Norman
was fond of his nephew, and had often said,
"Thank God, the boy is no fool;" but he
knew by repute what a very pretty and
attractive woman Mrs. Kynaston was, and
in his own vernacular he could not help
thinking that the pair might be a little
too much for any "young one," be he
never so clever. He had not heard of
Bertie for some time, and was far too good
a judge, if he really had got intimate with
these Kynastons, to interfere directly. But
he was not going to see his favourite
nephew plucked and made a fool of either;
and it was notorious that many a plump
pigeon had emerged from the Kynaston
dovecot so utterly devoid of feathers that
his dearest friends stood aghast at the com-
pleteness of the operation. Gilbert Slade,
however, as we know, was in no such
danger as his uncle pictured. He had seen
nothing of Mrs. Kynaston since Lincoln

Races, and, though thinking her a very pretty and pleasant woman to talk to, had been by no means fascinated; he did not possess that inflammable and susceptible temperament that is so easily smitten with love-fever. His was one of those harder natures, somewhat slow to feel anything of that kind, but who, when they do succumb to the arrow of the rosy god, are wont to love with a strong earnestness not easily diverted from its purpose.

But, though Gilbert Slade would have freely acknowledged the charms of either Mrs. Kynaston or Miss Devereux, yet he had thought but little about them since he had wished them " good-bye." His regiment had moved, as he had said it would, up to the North from Aldershot, and the consequence was that Gilbert had been little in London this year.

The Kynastons had thrown up The Firs at the end of the hunting-season, and were now quietly established in a snug little

house in Mayfair. Mrs. Kynaston was a
woman who went a good deal into society;
there were people who declined to know
her, saying that her flirtations were rather
too numerous and pronounced for their
taste; but she had never committed herself
by causing a grave scandal, and in many
houses was a favoured guest. As for the
Major, he took his own way in London; he
was never seen with his wife, and rarely in
society; he had his own haunts and amusements, such as the club card-room, bachelor
dinners, little theatrical suppers, trips down
to suburban meetings, &c. He and his wife
certainly lived under the same roof, but
when in London saw very little of each
other—their dining *téle-à-téle* being a rare
occurrence, and the Major was not given
to entertaining. Mrs. Kynaston always
pleaded their poverty on this point; but,
for all that, it was notorious amongst her
intimates that she gave the nicest little
lunches possible. There were never, at the

outside, above half-a-dozen people, and there was no laboured profusion, but the three or four dishes were admirably cooked, and the wine always undeniable.

Norman Slade had been rather indignant at finding Major Kynaston amongst the people he had been asked to meet. He was by no means particular, and had met queer people at the dinner-table before now, but he had always disliked all he had heard about Kynaston, and when they met he conceived an actual antipathy to him. He was a man strong in his dislikes, and it so happened the Major had been placed next him on this occasion. Kynaston, for his own purposes, had grossly exaggerated his acquaintance with Gilbert, which was, in reality, of the very slightest, as he had seen but little of him on the one occasion of their meeting. Like most of his class, he had a tremendous idea of his own astuteness; he was always vaunting that nobody ever got over Dick Kynaston, and fell, as

such men invariably do, into the mistake of
thinking he could turn his fellows inside
out. He thought Norman Slade might give
him many a valuable hint in Turf matters.
He had heard of that gentleman's reputation for reticence, but only let him—Dick
Kynaston—make his acquaintance, and he
would very soon worm out of him what he
knew.

Norman Slade literally swelled with in-
dignation at that dinner, when, under an
affectation of boisterous jocularity, he recognised that the Major was actually attempt-
ing to pump him! Can you fancy what the
feelings of a crack leader at the Old Bailey
would be at being cross-examined by Mr.
Briefless? But after a while Norman began
to take a saturnine pleasure in the operation, though the Major would have been
hardly re-assured could he have heard
Slade's remark to himself as he walked
home:

" If that chattering beast puts together all

he has got out of me, he'll find it amounts
to very little, and is more calculated to mis-
lead him than not."

The Major, on the contrary, went home
with the impression that he had quite sub-
dued the slight prejudice against him on
the part of Norman Slade to commence
with; that he had parted with that gentleman on the most friendly terms, and had
already possessed himself to some slight extent with Slade's views on forthcoming Turf
events. We do at times go home pluming
ourselves on the favourable impression we
have produced, serenely unconscious that
our host and hostess may have mutually
agreed that as it was the first so should it
be the last time we are present at their hospitable board. There is no end to the limit
of human vanity, and the people who
honestly recognise that they have, to use a
slang phrase, not "come off" in a social
gathering are few and far between. Most
of us believe that it is our jest or repartee

that gave brilliancy to the meeting, or that
it was our never being vouchsafed an opportunity clothed the gathering with such un-
mitigated dulness. No man had a higher
opinion of himself as a conversationalist
than the Major. He had a good stock of
stories, and not hackneyed stories, which he
told well, and he had a jovial off-hand sort
of manner, very apt to impose upon those
who were not shrewd observers. He never
made a greater mistake than when he
thought he had imposed upon Norman
Slade. That gentleman, who had carefully
avoided knowing him for some years, was
never so thoroughly convinced of the cor-
rectness of his judgment as at this moment.

Suddenly a tall, haggard-looking man
stopped abruptly opposite Norman, and with
a curt, " How d'ye do, Slade ? " sat himself
down on the adjacent chair. The merest
novice could have made no mistake about
the status of the newcomer. He was undoubtedly a man about whose position in

the world there could be little doubt, though the worn and haggard face was that of a man who, though still in his prime, was living a life that must break the strongest constitution if persisted in. The dark circles under the eyes, and the careworn lines about the mouth, were indicative of a man who kept abnormal hours, and never ceased battling with fortune, and his face did not belie him—play in some shape was pretty much Sir Ronald Radcliffe's idea of existence.

"Nice morning, Slade," he said, as he settled himself in a chair. "Not often you come amongst the trees and the dickey-birds, and you're about right. Awful bore, you know, if it's only the taking your hat off. Don't know why I come here, knowing such a lot of women as I do. Heard anything of old Bill Smith lately?"

"Yes," said Norman, gravely. "I'd a few lines from him not long ago, in which he said he had small hopes of his half-dozen

two-year-olds this year, that they were all
backward, and he believed most of them bad
—in short, I am afraid, Radcliffe, that Bill
has gone to the deuce. There isn't such a
horseman on the Turf, there isn't such a
juuge in a trial in England, but I hear from
up in the North that they can trust him no
longer. I don't mean that he isn't square
enough, but that drink has laid hold of him,
and there's no depending on his being sober
when wanted."

"End of everything when it comes to
that," said Sir Ronald. "A fellow gets mis-
taking the winning-post and all sorts of
games."

"Ah, well," said Slade, dreamily, "you
and I, Radcliffe, have landed many a pretty
coup out of poor old Bill's inspirations. I
shall go up and stay with him about the
back end, and I'll slip you a line then, and
tell you what I think of him. As for the
horses, I don't suppose his young ones are
worth looking at."

"It's getting about time I had a turn over something," replied the baronet, moodily. " Money is getting scarce as corn was in the bad times of Pharaoh. Don't know how the deuce you manage, Norman; things never seem to fly up and hit you in the face."

" Well, Radcliffe," rejoined Slade, " I neither bet nor spend money like you— haven't got it, and never had it, so I can't. I go for a *coup* now and again, as you know, but then it is on the strength of very excellent information, and I always stand to win a good stake at comparatively a small risk. My usual betting is a thing that never makes me uncomfortable, and, as for my whist, shillings and half-crowns content me."

" By Jove!" said Sir Ronald, turning half round in his chair, and surveying his companion in languid astonishment. " What a deuce of a lot of time you must have to spare. Why it would take you hours, and be a sinful waste of luck, to collect a few pounds at that price."

"Never you mind," rejoined Slade; "I only play for amusement."

" Of course, so does everybody; whist is a healthy recreation. My dear Norman, beware of indolence; and whist, for such pitiful points as you mention, is a waste of those golden hours concerning which that impostor the bee is always dangled before our eyes. Don't know much about that insect myself, but a fellow conversant with his habits told me the other day that the bee was nothing like such a fool as these ballad-mongers made him out; that when he had the chance he infinitely preferred stealing honey from the nearest grocer's to toiling for it on his own account."

" Well, Radcliffe," rejoined Slade, "you and I are old friends, and I'm not likely to leave you out in the cold whenever I get a chance. You can work a commission as well as anybody, and I know, from ex-

perience, don't cackle. But, honestly, at
the present moment, I know nothing more
than most racing men about coming events;
and as for what you want, a real good
chance at long odds, have no conception of
such a thing."

"Well," rejoined the Baronet, "much
obliged to you for your good opinion, old
man. The financial crisis presents its con-
stantly-recurring aspect; but there's nothing more to be done than, in the words of
the ballad, 'Fear not, but trust in Providence,' and devoutly hope my creditors will
trust in me;" and with this Sir Ronald
picked himself out of his chair, and, with a
slight nod to his companion, strolled on-
wards.

"Good fellow that!" muttered Slade;
"and, for all his swagger and languid airs,
just as 'cute a man about racing as I know.
They tell me he plays a capital rubber,
besides; but it must all beat him at last.
He's an extravagant man, and perpetually

playing for stakes out of all proportion to his capital. I wonder what Sir Ronald began the world with. He had a fair income, no doubt, to start with, but I should think he has reduced it a good deal since he came into the property, and, from all accounts, her ladyship is not likely to make his income go further."

As for the subject of these remarks, he strolled in his usual listless fashion towards Hyde Park Corner, exchanging greetings right and left on his way. Everybody seemed to know him, and with everyone did he seem popular. Women smiled and bowed to him with *empressement ;* men greeted him heartily, and not with that careless nod that signifies utter indifference at meeting one. Radcliffe was as popular a man as any in London; but how he had lasted so long with his extravagant habits was an enigma that puzzled those who knew him best extremely.

CHAPTER VII.

FURZEDON ENTERS SOCIETY.

"WELL, Lettice, I am very glad to have you with me again, though I don't quite know how I shall amuse you now you are here."

"Nonsense, auntie," rejoined Miss Devereux, laughing. "You London people always seem to us country folks to go out so much. I am sure when I pass six weeks with you I go out more than I do in all the remaining weeks of the year."

"I am a sociable being," laughed Mrs. Connop; "and, as Providence has given me the wherewithal to keep up a good house, I like to see people about. I like to see

young people, too, about me. It keeps one
from getting rusty, and I have no idea of
settling down into an old woman before my
time."

Nobody, certainly, would have described
Mrs. Connop as an old lady. She carried
her fifty years wonderfully well; without
affecting any undue juvenility, she was as
sprightly a woman of her age as any in
London; fond of society, full of go, and a
fluent talker, she had got together a large
if somewhat mixed acquaintance. She went
everywhere, and, though it is quite possible
that fastidious people would have pronounced her not in society, she mixed freely
in an extensive social world of her own.
She might be unrecognised by the queens of
the fashionable world, but there are various
circles in London that exchange the most
friendly relations, although their names
never figure in the *Morning Post*. A young
lady under Mrs. Connop's chaperonage
would be certain to have a good time of it,

although, perhaps, she would not be seen in
the stately mansions of Belgravia. Lettie
made no disguise about it: she always
looked forward eagerly to an invitation to
Onslow Gardens.

The Devereuxes were an energetic family,
and never allowed themselves to be bored
anywhere; they were people who could
always make for themselves occupation;
and, although North Leach was a quiet-
enough place when the hunting-season was
over, yet Miss Devereux never found her
time hang heavily on her hands. Still Lettie
invariably regarded her London visit as one
of the best "bits" in her year. There was,
too, just a little bit of uncertainty about it,
that gave a zest to the invitation. Although
her aunt had asked her regularly since she
had left school, yet there was always a possibility that that enterprising lady might
take it into her head to go abroad for a
time. This year Lettie was looking forward
to seeing a good deal of the Kynastons while

in town; she did not care very much about
the Major, but she had struck up a great
friendship with Mrs. Kynaston. That lady
reciprocated the feeling. There was a fresh
ness about Lettie which, though it a little
amused her, she could not but regret the
loss of in herself. Married to a man like
the Major, she had not been likely to retain
that quality long; and there were times
when Kate Kynaston felt bitterly sick of
the life she was condemned to lead. The
only daughter of fashionable but impecu-
nious parents, it had been impressed upon
her from her childhood that she was bound
to marry the first eligible suitor that presented himself. Captain Kynaston, as he
was then, a fast young man in a crack
Dragoon regiment, and with the reputation
of considerably more money than he had
ever possessed, seemed to Kate's father to
fulfil all reasonable expectations. It is true,
when they came to the settlements, that
battered old *roué* felt somewhat disap-

pointed, but things had gone too far to retract, and he could do no more than see that such settlement as Kynaston could or would make was tightly tied up. There is much virtue in a settlement to gentlemen of the Kynaston type, as it not uncommonly becomes to them after a few years the sole source of income upon which they can confidently rely. The Major's case was not exactly so bad as that, but with his tastes for good living, the card-table, and the race-course, his income, outside that settled on his wife, might be termed a little precarious.

There were people who spoke slightingly and shook their heads over Kate Kynaston's doings, although civil enough to her when they met. Kate's audacity sometimes paralysed them, and Kate's quick tongue undoubtedly awed them. She was a dangerous woman to splinter lances with; she had a quick eye for the joints in her adversary's harness; she mixed much in the world, and was thoroughly *au courant* with all the fashionable scandal of that world; and the quick, rapier-like thrust she could deliver under a traducer's guard had made women wondrous shy of personally attacking her. But, for all that, there were times when Kate tired bitterly of this ceaseless battle of life—of this continuous struggle to hold her own in the weary treadmill of society. It is all very well if you are one of the heavy galleons that sail under a recognised flag, but for the dashing privateers that flaunt their own gay colours, and only hold their own by finesse, adroitness, and cajolery, its fruits savour of the Dead Sea.

Kate Kynaston was just the woman who in the last century might have renounced all pomps and vanities, and betaken herself to a convent, might also very probably have got painfully bored with the seclusion in six months, emerged again into the world, and become more *mondaine* than ever; but in the days of which I am writing this was not to be thought of; moreover, the Major,

if he had no great regard for his wife, would
have been the last man to permit anything
of that sort. Mrs. Kynaston usually assented to his wishes with easy indifference,
but the Major had a dim perception that
there might come a time when some point
would raise a battle royal between them,
and that, should such arise, Kate might
prove troublesome to coerce.

It is singular how we re-act upon each
other's destinies; we go along on our own
jog-trot road till suddenly some new being,
of whose existence we have so far never
heard, crosses our path, and changes the
whole current of our destiny. Impossible
to say what this new factor in the woof of
our lives may do for us, but so it is; his
advent changes our fate for good or evil.
Mr. Furzedon, a few months ago, was
utterly unknown, even by name, to all the
characters in this story ; even Charlie
Devereux, whose acquaintance with him was
the longest, had known him scarce eighteen

months; and yet this man is destined to considerably affect most of the leading characters in this narrative. Mr. Furzedon has left Cambridge, not seeing his way into getting much more profit out of that University. He gave some very extensive wine and supper parties previous to his departure, at which no expense was spared. As before said, he was a man who could spend money freely when he saw a possible return for doing so. And in this instance he was anxious to thoroughly clinch his acquaintance with all the eligible young men he had contrived to get intimate with.

Mr. Furzedon has established himself in chambers in Ryder Street, and, as he sits lingering over a latish breakfast, is meditating deeply how he is to set about the working his way into society of some sort. A shrewd, pushing man, callous to a rebuff, and of considerable tenacity of purpose, he was pretty certain to attain his end before long. As he had gone to the University for the sole purpose of making desirable acquaintance, so he had lately contrived to get himself elected to a club. It was not, perhaps, one of the crack establishments of the West End, but had a fair second-rate reputation, and its ballot was known to be not so stringent as in some possessed of greater *prestige*. Like even the best of clubs, its members were rather a mixed lot. Mr. Furzedon frequented the Parthian with great assiduity; he set himself to work to learn the names and history of the members, and it is astonishing how much a man who makes that kind of thing his business can pick up about his brethren. There are clubs of which it is said : " They never let the wrong man in there." Sheer fallacy! The most exclusive coterie, like any other community, cannot avoid falling into that mistake. If at times institutions like the Parthian, owing to a shortness of members, are not quite so strict in their ballot, it naturally follows that the proportion of black sheep is larger, and it was in sifting the black from the white that Mr. Furzedon was now engaged. The conduct of clubmen is erratic; there is the pleasant, genial, talkative man, known to every one, but of whose life nobody can tell anything after he has passed the club porter; there is the man who dines there three hundred nights out of the year, but who apparently knows nobody, and invariably takes his meal in solitude; there is the member who bores you with his own affairs; there is the irascible member who is in weekly communication with the Committee.

It was not likely that Furzedon could arrive at a sketch of the lives of all of his brethren, but he did of a great many. He himself was merely a representative of a type found in all similar institutions, the man who invariably calls the waiters and inquires the name of any one whose face he does not know .Where Furzedon thought his inquiries satisfactory he endeavoured to scrape an acquaintance. This brings us again to another type of club man, not quite such a bore, perhaps, as Toe Thompson, who, as the legend goes, always commenced his insidious advances by treading on his victim's corns and then apologising, but Mr. Furzedon was conscious that he must do something more than that. Club acquaintance by no means leads to intimacy with social surroundings. He was busy this morning thinking what houses he could call at, and Mr. Furzedon felt gloomily that, with the end he had in view, they were very circumscribed in number. There was Mrs. Kynaston, but then he did not know were she was. She was a lady with no fixed abode, and, though she and the Major usually spent six months of their year in town, yet they rented their house as they chanced to pick it up. Ah! there was Mrs. Connop, that was the aunt Miss Devereux always came to stay with, and surely Miss Devereux must be in town by now. No difficulty in finding Mrs. Connop, she had a permanent abode, her address was easily to be arrived at in the Blue Book, and if he could only see Miss Devereux, she would probably know were Mrs. Kynaston resided.

Adhering to his plan, Mr. Furzedon made his way out towards South Kensington that afternoon, and in Piccadilly he passed Gilbert Slade. Now he had never seen that gentleman, except at Lincoln races, and the Slades as a race were not people who knew you lightly. Furzedon, even on that occasion, had hardly exchanged half-a-dozen words with him, but, constant to the principle he had laid down, he nevertheless nodded genially to Gilbert. That gentleman's face simply expressed blank recognition, and then he returned the salutation by slightly touching his hat. Gilbert Slade, in good truth, had no recollection of who it was that had bowed to him; but Mr. Furzedon had two points invaluable to him in the *rôle* he proposed to play—he had a capital memory for both names and faces.

That afternoon witnessed the *début* of Mr. Furzedon in Onslow Gardens. The defunct pawnbroker's son had, at all events, mastered one of the mysteries of fashion; he had learnt how to knock. One may think the knocking at a door is of no consequence, perhaps not to the proprietors of the house, who may or may not hear it, and who very likely, if they do, pay little attention to it. I am not going to enter into that vast question so intelligible to those conversant with the history of the knocker, to whom the knock of the post, the dun, the taxes, the begging petitioner, the borrower, the wealthy but exasperated relative. &c., are as easy to read as telegrams. I am alluding only to the visitor's knock. And in the servants' hall this is interpreted on a mutely acknowledged scale accordingly. On those of the nervous, timid, and hesitating knock, they invariably bestow arrogance and contumely, but to the donor of the bold, audacious roulade on the knocker they are invariably cap in hand. Delicious are the errors into which these clumsy menials constantly fall, except they are servants of the very best class: the swaggering manner and a certain gorgeousness of dress will constantly impose upon them. They kootoo to the confident stock-broker, and turn up their noses at the more diffident peer.

Mr. Furzedon, in all the gorgeousness of his summer raiment, preceded by his dashing peal on the knocker, was just the sort of man that quiet servitors would be startled by. There was nothing *outré* about his garments, but everybody will understand what I mean when I say that they were just a little too glossy. It is difficult to explain, but a well-dressed man of the world never seems to put on a new coat. Furzedon was wont to have the appearance of having received his clothes only the night before from his tailor.

Yes, Miss Devereux was staying there, and Mrs. Connop would be very glad to see Mr. Furzedon, was the answer that came down in acknowledgment of his card. Mr. Furzedon lost no time in responding to the invitation, and as he entered the drawing-room Lettice advanced to meet him, and, after shaking hands with him, at once presented him to her aunt.

"Very glad, indeed, Mr. Fursedon, to make your acquaintance. I am always pleased to see any friends of my family; and Lettie tells me that you have been staying at North Leach all the winter, and are now quite a known man with the Brocklesby."

"I am afraid Miss Devereux is a little laughing at me when she says that. I certainly can claim in one sense to be a well-known man in that country, namely, that I was a constant attendant at their meets, and had capital good fun; but a well-known man is usually translated into a very promi-nent horseman with such hounds. I am afraid I wasn't quite that. They were all a little too good for me down there."

" Ah, auntie, you must not trust to this mock humility. Mr. Furzedon held his own with most of us."

" Very good of you to say so, Miss Deve-reux, and I'll not be such a fool as to argue that view of the case with you. Anyway, Mrs. Connop, I had a capital time at North Leach, and two very jolly days at Lincoln afterwards, although, sad to say, the family banner—that is metaphorical for colours, you know—was not triumphant."

" Never mind," exclaimed Mrs. Connop; " I wasn't born a Devereux without know-ing something of these things. I didn't see it, but Charlie's young, and I'll go bail he does better yet. From my recollection of all those cheery Hunt Steeplechases, the young ones were very apt to get a little the worst of it at first, but a few years' practice and they turn the tables. There is no truer adage, Mr. Furzedon, than that youth will be served. I don't call myself an old woman, and never mean to, but if you ask me whether Lettie can walk me down—well —I suspect she can."

" No," said Furzedon; " nobody ever does grow old in these days. Why, look at all our leading public men—boys still, in spite of what their baptismal registers assert to the contrary. By the way, Miss Devereux, have you seen anything of the Kynastons since you have been in town ? "

" Not as yet," rejoined Lettie, " but I have only been here three days as yet. In fact, I am rather surprised at your having heard of my arrival."

" Well," replied Furzedon, " that is a pure piece of good fortune on my part. I remember that you said in the winter you very often spent a few weeks with Mrs.

Connop about this time of the year, so I thought I would call."

".Charlie tells me you have done with Cambridge."

" Yes," rejoined Furzedon; " I never intended to take a degree, but my guardians were right—it is good for a man to go to the University for a time. It opens his eyes, and gives him a glimpse of the world."

Mr. Furzedon's guardians were shadowy people, to whom he only alluded when it suited his purpose. They had interfered very little indeed with him, and the going to Cambridge had been entirely his own idea, and of his object in doing so we are already aware. He had been, moreover, of age now some little time, and was consequently emancipated from the very light control his guardians had ever attempted to exercise. After a little more desultory talk, Mr. Furzedon rose to take his leave, and received from Mrs. Connop, as he did so, a cordial intimation that she would be glad to see him whenever he chose to call. He had also learnt from Lettice that the Kynastons had taken a house in Chester Street, Mayfair.

" Not a bad beginning," thought Mr. Furzedon, as he strolled eastwards. " I've got my foot fairly inside that house, and it will be my own fault if I don't establish myself on Mrs. Connop's visiting list. Mrs. Kynaston, too, can be a very useful woman to me if she likes. I don't suppose that they entertain much, but I fancy they have a very numerous acquaintance in London, and that Mrs. Kynaston could introduce one pretty widely if she chose."

CHAPTER VIII.

LADY RAMSBURY'S GARDEN-PARTY.

MORE hospitable people than the Ramsburys never existed. They lived in a
great red brick house in Chelsea—one of
those modern imitations of the old Eliza-
bethan style of house such as you may
see in Pont Street. It stood in the midst
of a large garden, and the Ramsburys
delighted in big dinners during the winter
months, and in large garden-parties in the
summer. What Sir John Ramsbury had
been knighted for was rather a mystery.
He was known as a " warm " man in the
City, was Alderman of his Ward, and, though
he had never passed the chair, it was

always regarded that was an honour he might aspire to any day. However, he had attained the distinction of knighthood, the why could be only explained otherwise than he had been the chairman of several commercial enterprises, supposed to have resulted in much benefit to the country, and, what was rather more to the point, in considerable benefit to Sir John Ramsbury.

Lady Ramsbury's "gardens" were a well-known feature in the London season. The company might be a little mixed, but there were plenty of right good people always to be found there. Sir John, as director of various companies, had come across a good deal of the salt of this earth, and in this latter half of the nineteenth century, when the struggle for existence waxes harder and harder, both to those with the bluest of blood in their veins and to those born in the gutter, the man with the capability of putting money into his friends' pockets is a power.

There has never been a time when fashion in pursuit of its follies did not grovel at the feet of Plutus. How our neighbours bowed down at the shrine of Law, and many of us can remember when to sit at the table of the railway king was matter of gratulation to half the best society in London. Who could whisper such auriferous secrets into dainty ears as he could? and, though irreverent guardsmen might put up their glasses at some of the social solecisms he was wont to commit, yet their seniors and the mothers that bore them were too worldly-wise not to overlook such trifles as those. In similar fashion, Sir John Ramsbury commanded a considerable number of guests at his parties. He did the thing right well; there was never any lack of everything of the best in the commissariat department at his parties, and it must, in justice to the worthy knight and his lady, be added that they were unconventional people, but by no means vulgar.

Lady Ramsbury and Mrs. Connop were old friends; the lamented Connop had been mixed up with various business speculations in Sir John's early days, before he blossomed into knighthood and the dignity of a house at Chelsea, so that there was nothing singular in Lettie and her aunt finding themselves in that pleasant old garden one fine June afternoon.

After shaking hands with their hostess, Mrs. Connop and her niece began to slowly pace the lawn. They met plenty of acquaintance, and were enjoying themselves in a careless, gossiping way, when Lettie's eye was caught by a group of three people who were occupying a garden-bench, and conversing somewhat earnestly. The centre of the group, and the person who had first attracted her attention, was a slight, elderly man, with a decided stoop, and an eye like a hawk. Seated on one side of him was a stout elderly lady, richly dressed, but who evidently considered that Nature was a handmaid to Art. The merest tyro would have known her colour was not that of fresh air and superabundant life, and made a shrewd guess that her exuberant tresses came straight from her hairdresser's. But Lady Melfort was a well-known and very popular person. Ascot or Newmarket, Epsom or Doncaster, would have seemed incomplete without the presence of that dashing and evergreen Countess. On the other was Gilbert Slade. As far as Lettie could see, the conversation rested principally with the lady, who was declaiming volubly, while Norman Slade, who was the central figure of the group, merely threw in an interjectional word now and again.

Norman Slade had no objection to fighting the Turf battles of bygone days over again with any one who really understood racing, and the sporting peeress, who was a thorough enthusiast, was by no means a bad judge.

"I don't agree with you, Lady Melfort,"

he ejaculated, in reply to some story of her ladyship's, the gist of which appeared to be that she had lost her money when she thought she ought to have won it. " It is true, on his previous form the horse ought to have won, but it by no means follows that there was any foul play connected with his running; horses, like ourselves, are not always quite themselves, and the cleverest trainer sometimes fails to detect that his charge is a little off. I know that people connected with Lucifer backed him upon that occasion."

" I should like to know what his jockey did," rejoined her ladyship, sharply.

" His best, I think," rejoined Norman ; "he's a steady, civil boy enough, and we are rather too apt to make the jockey answerable for the shortcomings of the horse."

But her ladyship was evidently not convinced, she was given to be somewhat suspicious of unfair play when her racing calculations proved fallible.

At this juncture Gilbert caught sight of Miss Devereux, and, as he was by no means such an enthusiast about the "sport of kings" as his companions, he at once raised his hat and proceeded to join her.

"How d'ye do, Miss Devereux? Rather different weather from that when I last saw you. How long have you been in town?"

"Only about a week," rejoined Lettie; "but let me introduce you to my aunt, Mrs. Connop, with whom I am staying."

Gilbert bowed, and muttered something about "doing himself the pleasure of calling;" and then, turning to Lettie, said, "I suppose now you'll see the season out?"

"Oh, yes," replied the girl. "I want to go everywhere and do everything, see all there is to be seen, and meet all my friends. I suppose, Mr. Slade, that your intentions are somewhat similar."

"Ah! it doesn't signify what my intentions may be. When you're a soldier, you find the Horse Guards interfere with such things in ruthless fashion. No; I regret to say that I only got a month's leave, and that a week of it is already gone. Has Polestar won his spurs yet, Miss Devereux?"

"No," rejoined Lettie; "how can you recall that day of disgrace to me?"

"Not disgrace," rejoined Gilbert; "you were defeated, as we all are at times; but, I fancy, if the race had been run over again, your brother would have made a closer thing of it?"

"Ah! I daresay Charlie will have another opportunity of distinguishing himself in the autumn. Is there any likelihood of your being present at the autumn meeting on the Carholme?"

"It is very likely," rejoined Gilbert. "I am quartered at York, and I should think it is easy to slip down from there. However, it is a long way off as yet."

"Who was that gentleman you were talking to, Mr. Slade?" inquired Miss Devereux.

"That was my uncle Norman," replied Gilbert. "It is not often that he leaves his usual haunts for anything of this sort; but, for some reason, he is very fond of the Ramsburys—he has known them a good many years; and I've a vague suspicion that Sir John did him a kindness at some period of his life. All I know is, that, though he is a real good fellow, my uncle Norman is peculiar, and it is by no means every one that could lure him to their dinner-table; not many people, I fancy, who would have got him to do a thing of this kind."

"I am sure it is charming," replied Miss Devereux, laughing; "such pretty grounds, so many people, and such a good band to listen to; I don't think your good uncle is much to be pitied."

"No," said Gilbert; "but people differ in taste, and this is not much in my uncle Norman's line." And the conversation turned upon military affairs; for, not a

little to Gilbert's surprise, Miss Devereux
manifested no small curiosity anent "soldiering." It was easy of explanation.
During the winter she and her brother
Charlie had had many a talk together as
to what line of life he was to pursue, and
he had more than once spoken seriously of
the army as a profession calculated to suit
him when his career at Cambridge was done
with. Letty warmly approved of that determination. She had a very vague idea of
what a soldier's life was like; but thought
that a man who was a good horseman ought
to make a likely dragoon.

Norman Slade continued to talk in his
lazy way to Lady Melfort. The Countess
always amused him, while he usually acted
as a pleasing irritant upon her. He listened
to her vehement protestations of the iniqui-
ties of the Turf with a quiet smile, and
invariably exasperated her by claiming a
high position for the main part of those
connected with it, and declaring that people

who lose a little money shrieked and made bitter wail over the treachery that they had encountered, forgetting about the extreme uncertainty that distinguishes racing beyond even most mundane affairs.

"My dear Countess," he would say, "you don't rail against M. Blanc when you lose your money at Monte Carlo, and yet when you come to gambling on the Turf—and you know, Lady Melfort, you are a gambler— you don't bet merely upon the races you understand and can form an opinion about, but you bet on all sorts of handicaps and selling races, of which, concerning the merits of the competitors, you know nothing.''

"Well, I hate to see a race, Mr. Slade, without having something on it."

"Just so," rejoined Norman; "then you couldn't bear to see the ball spinning round at Monte Carlo without having a stake on it, and, whether you back the red or the black, it is just about as great a lottery as some of these races you speculate on."

If Norman somewhat irritated her, Lady Melfort had a profound respect for his judgment. She believed him to be able to elucidate many a Turf mystery that had puzzled racing-people profoundly, and in this she was right; there were few men perhaps more behind the scenes than Norman Slade. There were not many Turf robberies of which he could not explain the history. Pray don't think for one moment he was a participator in them. Like the general public, he had occasionally been a victim; but, when the scandal connected with such events was once blown over, a story in Turf circles is pretty certain to leak out in more or less accurate form, and he sometimes regaled Lady Melfort with the true history of one of these bygone surprises. Like many men of his type, good-hearted fellow though he was at bottom, he would hardly have interfered to save any one in whom he was not interested from being awfully taken advantage of.

"It is wonderful," he was wont to say, "the amount of foolishness there is in this world, and, as regards racing, the man who undertook the task of being guardian to the dovecot would have a thankless and onerous office. These 'squabs,' if they have any independence, emerged from the parental dwelling with a complacent self-sufficiency no warning could disturb."

He would have interfered fast enough on behalf of his favourite nephew had he seen occasion, but Gilbert was a man quite able to take care of himself, and with no taint of gambling in his blood. Norman in his varied life had seen young men come to grief from various causes, and had more than once, at the instigation of anxious relatives, interfered in their behalf. One rule he always firmly adhered to. "Don't ask me," he would say, "to meddle in the affairs of a young gentleman who is going down hill at a hand-gallop. I don't like young gentlemen—their talk bores me, and they don't like me. They are sure not to take my advice, and call me an old fogey, I've no doubt, when my back is turned. However, when your hopeful has gone a 'real perisher' I will step in if you wish it. The young man in difficulties, and the young man with his quill-feathers still un-plucked, are very different people to deal with."

Miss Devereux and Gilbert Slade con-tinued to improve their acquaintance during the best part of the afternoon. The young lady had not a very numerous acquaintance present, and was not at all averse to having this good-looking hussar dangling by her side. Gilbert thought her, as he well might, a very pretty girl. He had not been so much struck with her at Lincoln, but now she was arrayed in all her summer braveries he freely acknowledged her beauty, and, what was more to the point, her lively talk amused him. It was not that he did not know plenty of people, for many a fair head was bent in salutation to him as he paced the grass by Lettie's side, but Gilbert was too pleased with his present companion to seek for change—in fact, by the time he had put Mrs. Connop and her niece into their carriage it was quite arranged that he should call in Onslow Gardens the next day.

" She is rather a nice girl, that," mused Mr. Slade, as he paced homewards with a vigilant eye for a passing hansom; " besides, after the way in which her mother lunched me at Lincoln, I am bound to make my obeisance to the young lady and her aunt. What splendid brown eyes she has—and what a figure for a riding-habit! "

I fancy those eyes had much to say to Gilbert's punctilious politeness, for had Miss Devereux been other than she was he would not so clearly have recognised the necessity of calling in Onslow Gardens. He was a young man apt to be a little careless of such social obligations, but, though very far from impressionable, he had always a genuine admiration for a pretty woman, and was fond of women's society. He differed from both his uncles in that respect, who, though leading very different lives, were alike in that one thing—they both eschewed the society of the fair sex, except upon rare occasions.

Miss Devereux, as she drove along, looked back on a very pleasant afternoon. "Charlie must be a soldier," she thought, "I rather like soldiers." And then Lettie could not help laughing as she considered how very limited her military acquaintance was—Mr. Slade, and two or three officers whom she had danced with at Hunt Balls—and had no recollection of being particularly impressed with at the time. She was conscious herself that she was basing her predilection for the army entirely upon Gilbert Slade, whom, after all, she had only met three times. Major Kynaston, the only soldier of whom she had much knowledge, she undoubtedly had but little admiration for, but then she decided in her own mind that he was probably an unfavourable specimen.

Suddenly Mrs. Connop exclaimed, with some abruptness, "When did you hear from Charlie last?"

"Oh, not for some days."

"Where do you suppose he is?" inquired her aunt.

"He is sure to be at Cambridge."

"I don't think he is, my dear," rejoined Mrs. Connop. "I forgot to tell you, but when I was out shopping this morning, Charlie passed me in a hansom cab, unless I am very much mistaken."

"Did he see you, auntie?"

"No; of that I am quite sure. It is very odd he should be in town and not come out to see me."

Miss Devereux made no reply. It was not very likely that her aunt was mistaken, and she knew that Mrs. Connop much resented any of her family not duly present-

ing themselves in Onslow Gardens on such
occasions, while Lettie was also aware that
young gentlemen at the University were not
uncommonly in London without the knowledge of their relations. She kept her misgivings carefully to herself, but from a little
that had escaped Charlie in the winter she
felt pretty sure that there were money
troubles impending over his head, and that
the storm was likely to burst at any
moment.

CHAPTER IX.

A LITTLE GAME AT BILLIARDS.

IT is a curious thing, but it is nevertheless most generally the case, that when a young gentleman gets into difficulties he is apt to bestow his confidence, and take advice, in all probability from the very last man he should select. To go to the home authorities, undoubtedly the best people in whom to confide until by repetition their patience has been exhausted, is about the last thing that occurs to many of us in those days of hot youth and difficulties. Charlie Deve-reux had got a bit dipped at the University, but it was not that which troubled him; he could have carried such debts as those

straight to his father without fear of his
reception. He might be called "an extravagant young dog," and there might be a
good bit of grumbling over it, still he knew
they would be paid. But Furzedon had
gradually imbued him with a taste for
racing and the backing of horses at Newmarket. Charlie was of far too impulsive a
disposition ever to do much good in that
way. A man may be a very fine horseman,
or, even more, he may be a very fair judge
of racing, and yet have no manner of dis-
cretion in the backing of horses. Charlie
in the first place had been indebted to
Furzedon for the means with which to meet
his liabilities, but as he got intimate with
the Kynastons he was, like many another
young man before him, very much impressed
by the Major's apparent knowledge of the
world.

The Major always did impose upon young
men in this wise. A man who really does
believe in himself is very apt to imbue his

fellows with like belief, and, despite many rude shocks that should have shaken his opinion, Kynaston still prided himself upon his astuteness. There was not a "leg" at Newmarket that he was not more than a match for; the cleverest adventurer in London would never get the best of him at either the billiard or the card-table. As for the Stock Exchange, they knew a thing or two there, but they would have to get up very early in the morning to get the best of Dick Kynaston.

Dining at The Firs one night after a capital day's hunting, when the Major had suggested that just a couple of glasses of port apiece could not possibly hurt them after such a glorious gallop in the open, Charlie had made a clean breast of his troubles to his host. The latter listened with great interest. Young men's difficulties always had an interest for him. His knowledge of money-brokers and bill-discounters was extensive, and nobody understood the rights

of salvage better than he did. He delighted
in being hailed by the sinking ship when
the skipper was young, and too thankful for
his help to dream of disputing the price of
his redemption. Very pretty pickings to be
had in these cases, the Major knew. Of
course there were others who must be permitted to share in the spoils; but the Major
was a jackal of mark, and by no means,
when the picking of the carcass took place,
to be put off with bare bones.

He told Charlie that he had no doubt he
could help him, but he would take a little
time to consider of it, which, being interpreted, meant that Dick Kynaston intended
leisurely to appraise his victim. It was not,
remember, that he had won any money from
Charlie, but that the latter had come to him
with the story of his difficulties. When the
Major came to consider the speculation, he
considered it might probably turn out a profitable one. To begin with, the Devereuxes
were unmistakeably well-to-do people, and

that, therefore, the money was certain to be all right in the long-run—a thing that the gentleman to whom he meant to confide the relief of Charlie's necessities would be doubtless anxious about. Secondly, he thought there was nothing more probable than that from this, as yet, embryo North Leach stable might spring a dangerous steeplechaser or two, and to be behind the scenes in such case might be the means of putting several hundreds into his pocket. Lastly, like Mr. Furzedon, Kynaston recognised that Charlie had the makings of a real horseman—a little green, perhaps, at present, but only wanting practice to develop into a first-class gentleman rider. Acting on all this, the Major had enabled Charlie to discharge his debt to Furzedon and save his hunters, but it had all been done in the usual way— bills of six months, bearing ruinous interest, which Charlie had signed, with the Major's rollicking assurance ringing in his ears, of—

" Pooh, my dear boy! we shall have one

or two more rolls of the ball before these come due, and you will probably win a nice little stake on one of the Spring handicaps, which will enable you to just light cigars with them."

There are people who have broken the bank at Homburg, and I suppose there are people in Charlie's circumstances who have won enough money to discharge similar liabilities, but to the ordinary run of humanity such a thing never happens, and when it does I, in the superstition engendered by long years of watching the battle of the gambler with fortune, fear every gruesome fate for him. One I knew, who, after steadily plodding through years of ill-luck on the Turf that might have deterred many men from continuing, at last had *his year*. He was no heavy gambler, but how much he won between the First Newmarket Spring and the finish of the Ascot week was preposterous, considering the stakes with which he originally started. That he had followed his luck there is no need to say, and had bet at Ascot in a way hitherto unknown to him; but it benefited him, poor fellow, but little, for ere the next twelve-month was over he was laid peacefully in his grave, and recked little of what went on on that Turf he had loved so dearly.

But those bills had at last become due, while that nice little stake which the Major had so jauntily predicted had not as yet been landed. Kynaston dropped a line to his young friend, and informed him that, unless he saw his way to meeting them, it was absolutely necessary he should come up to town and make arrangements for their renewal; and this it was that had brought Charlie Devereux to London. Kynaston determined to take advantage of the opportunity to give a little dinner to Devereux and Furzedon. The latter somewhat puzzled him. He was conscious that Furzedon was a shrewdish young gentleman, though he would naturally have derided the idea of

any one of *his* years getting the better of
Dick Kynaston. A thing that had rather
puzzled Furzedon had been where Charlie
had procured the money to settle with him;
but the Major had cautioned Devereux to
keep silence respecting those bill transactions, and, as Charlie had not volunteered
any information, Furzedon could not, of
course, press him on the subject. Kynaston
was not given to entertaining, and, like one
of his guests, usually had some object in
view when he did extend his hospitality;
but the tastes of young men who had either
money or well-to-do relatives he always
considered were worth studying. He had
gathered up in the wolds during the hunting-season that Charlie, amongst other
things, was a little proud of his billiard-
playing, but at The Firs, and upon the two
or three occasions that he had dined at
North Leach, there had been no opportunity
of testing young Devereux's skill in that
particular.

The Major's off-hand invitations to dine with him at the Thermopolium were both accepted, although Furzedon pleaded, in consequence of another engagement, that he should have to run away soon after dinner was over. Major Kynaston could be a good host when he chose to take the trouble, and the trio, after a satisfactory repast, lingered for some time over their wine. At last Furzedon declared he must go, and after his departure Kynaston proposed that they should have a game of billiards with their cigar. Charlie was delighted with the proposition, and, having adjourned to the strangers' billiard-room, they commenced their game. They happened to have the room to themselves, and at first seemed evenly matched, but towards the middle of the game Charlie began to draw away from his opponent, and apparently won pretty easily at the finish. Kynaston seemed a little nettled at this, proposed another game of a hundred up and offered to bet a crown he won it. He certainly made a better fight this time, but Devereux was once more victorious; still, the Major declined to own himself defeated, and suggested another game for the same nominal stake. Devereux assented, and even offered to give a few points, which the Major testily declined. This time the scoring ran pretty even, when a stout gentleman, smoking a very large cigar, lounged into the room, nodded slightly to Kynaston, and, seating himself on the adjacent bench, proceeded to watch the play. The arrival of the new comer seemed slightly to disconcert the Major, but, at the same time, it seemed to have improved his play. A somewhat amused expression stole over the looker-on's face; and, when Kynaston eventually proved the conqueror by a few points, he rose from his seat, and, as he sauntered out of the room, remarked—

"Hardly playing up to your usual form, Kynaston."

"Always the case," replied that gentleman, "when you drink champagne at
dinner; you never can quite tell what the
effect will be. You either play below your
game or a good many points above it."

"Perhaps so," rejoined Bob Braddock,
for it was he who had been the amused
spectator. "I don't know who that very
young gentleman is," he muttered to himself, as he left the room; "but, if he thinks
that he can form the slightest idea of Dick
Kynaston's game of billiards from what he
has seen to-night, he is very much mistaken.
I don't suppose he has any conception that
he has got hold of about the very best
player we have got amongst us, and whom
I fancy there are not half-a-dozen gentleman players in London can tackle."

Major Braddock was right; although
Charlie was no fool, he had not the slightest
idea, so well was it done, that Kynaston
was concealing his game; he looked upon
him as much such a player as himself; but

thought that he was a little the best of the
two. However, they played a couple more
games upon even terms, and, whatever
Kynaston's object might have been, it was
evident he had no design upon Charlie at
present; for in one of these games he was
easily beaten, and the other he just won by
an apparent fluke. Nor did he make the
slightest attempt to induce Charlie to bet
further than the modest stake first proposed.

Whether Mr. Furzedon, if he had re-
mained and witnessed the episode of the
billiard-playing, would have been much en-
lightened about his host's character, it is
hard to say. Furzedon was very shrewd,
no doubt, and it must be borne in mind
four years Devereux's senior; but it is very
difficult indeed, knowing nothing of a good
billiard-player's game, to know whether he
is doing his best; then, again, Furzedon
had never set himself to study Major Kynaston. He knew that he was a sporting-man,

much addicted to horseracing, and he had
little doubt with a taste for play; but he
had never troubled his head to take further
stock of him. He had dined with Kynaston
at some little inconvenience, simply with
the view of cementing the acquaintance
commenced at North Leach. He looked to
Mrs. Kynaston principally to help him in
the main ambition of his life, namely, the
working his way into London society. Mr.
Furzedon had a high idea of utilising his
fellows in anywise; but it had not so far
struck him that the Major could be useful
to him. He had not yet fathomed the vain-
glorious weakness of Kynaston's nature.
The Major never could resist vaunting his
triumphs when fortune favoured him, either
on the baize or on the grass.

Young Devereux regained his quarters
with all the complacency of a man who
has spent a thoroughly satisfactory evening.
He had had an excellent dinner, a good
tussle at billiards with an opponent worthy

of his steel, but of whom he firmly believed
he had legitimately got the best, and, crown-
ing mercy of all, the Major had told him
those bills would be comfortably arranged
for the present. It is true that there was
something bitter within the cup, and, young
and reckless as he was, even Charlie made
a wry face at the price he was told he
would have to pay for this further accom-
modation. Only he had a delicacy about
it, he had far better have taken Furzedon
into his confidence. Even if that gentleman had charged him interest for extend-
ing his loan, it would have been something
bearing a very mild proportion to what his
present benefactors required for their ser-
vices. As Mrs. Connop rightly surmised,
Charlie had not seen her. He was only
up for two or three days, and did not particularly wish his relations to know of his
presence in London, more especially Lettie.
He was very fond of his sister, knew that
her suspicions were already slightly aroused

about the state of his affairs, and was not
at all inclined to submit to her keen ques-
tioning. " No," he thought, " Lettie always
could worm anything out of me, and it's not
a bit of use worrying her with this scrape,
and she has all her life taken my troubles
a deuced deal more hardly than I ever did
myself. It is awkward, and if I can't win
a race with Pole star in the autumn I don't
see my way out of it. But Lettie's a real
good sort, and she shan't be bothered with
my troubles as long as I can help it.'

Miss Devereux, as we know, was already
anxious about her brother, and had she
known where to write to him would have
communicated with him at once, but Charlie
had not as yet attained to the dignity of a
club, and, though when in London he always
encamped in the vicinity of St. James's
church, the precise street as well as number
of the house were always uncertain. Duke
Street, Ryder Street, Bury Street, Jermyn
Street, &c., he had lodged in them all. At

this time of year rooms in that locality were
at a premium, and Miss Devereux knew that
it was more a case of getting in where you
could than where you chose. The only
person she could think of likely to know
Charlie's address was Mr. Furzedon, and
that gentleman, whether he found people
in or out, was much too wary not to leave
his card on the hall table. Lettie accordingly dropped a line to Mr. Furzedon at the
Parthian Club, asking for her brother's
address, or, should he come across him that
evening, would he tell him to call in Onslow
Gardens.

It was late before Kynaston left the
Thermopolium after his billiard tourna-
ment. He had accompanied Charlie downstairs, but at their foot encountered an old
chum whom he had not seen for many years,
had consented to turn into the smoking-
room on the ground floor, and have just
one small cigar and a chat over old times.
Bidding Charlie good night, he did this

" ancient mariner's " bidding, and, ah me ! how many of us can remember the dire headache that is the result of those chats about old times, how that small cigar and ...odest liquor accompaniment expands, and how " hearing the chimes at midnight " is a lukewarm jest in comparison with the chimes we do hear upon such occasion.   It is very late indeed as Kynaston prepared to emerge from the wicket of the Thermopolium. The big doors had been long since closed, and only that rabbit-like portal was open to the belated members. As the night-porter unlatched it for him he handed him a mean and dirty-looking note, which, after one glance at the superscription, the Major thrust carelessly into his waistcoat pocket.

CHAPTER X.

IN ONSLOW GARDENS.

"No, there's not much difficulty about it, and from what you tell me, Miss Devereux, I should think it is the very profession to suit your brother. There is an examination to pass, of course; but most of us manage to do that after being sharpened up by a coach for a few months."

"Yes; and Charles has had a University education," replied the young lady.

"Ah! they don't always bring much book-learning away from that," rejoined Gilbert Slade, laughing; "but they are not required to be so very deeply read to qualify for the service as yet. If your brother has made up his mind, he ought to lose no time about it. It's a pleasant life enough. The one drawback about it is that it is not a money-making profession."

" Well, Mr. Slade, I shall look to you to put us in the way of making Charlie a soldier."

" I am afraid they won't pay very much attention to the recommendation of a subaltern of dragoons ; but I might be of some use to you for all that, Miss Devereux. My uncle, familiarly known in the service as Bob Braddock—he was christened Henry, but a fellow who is good for anything always gets re-christened in his regiment—is hand-and-glove with all sorts of swells, and a nomination for a commission is not much to ask for."

" Ah! here comes auntie !" exclaimed Miss Devereux, as her quick ear detected a hand upon the door-handle. " Not a word about my brother," she added, hurriedly in

an undertone; "he is a little in disgrace
just now."

Mrs. Connop welcomed Gilbert cordially.
She was fond of young men, and always
did her best to make her house pleasant to
them. She had a critical eye for masculine
good looks, and Gilbert's tall muscular figure
and dark resolute face were of the type
she most admired. There was a touch of
romance about Mrs. Connop with which
only those who knew the good-tempered,
vivacious lady intimately would have
credited her.

Lettice understood her aunt thoroughly,
and knew that she revelled in sentimental
poetry; and that her eyes would even yet
moisten over the perusal of a thrilling love-
story.

"You have kept your promise, Mr. Slade,"
said Mrs. Connop, as she shook hands.
"And you will be so far rewarded in that
you will meet another of your sporting
acquaintance in a quarter of an hour or so.

I call them so," she continued, laughing,
" for, as far as I can make out, you, Lettie,
and Mrs. Kynaston have only met on the
racecourse."

"Not as yet," replied Slade; "but I trust
it will be different in future. I'm not at all
one of those men who spend the best part
of their lives in the pursuit of racing."

" It is exciting," exclaimed Lettie; " remember what a fever we were all in about
Charlie and Polestar at Lincoln."

"Exciting! Yes," replied Gilbert, quietly,
"you had special cause for it then. Nobody
appreciates and enjoys a good race when it
comes in my way more than I do; but it
is not to me what it is to my uncle Norman, for instance—the very breath of his
nostrils."

"May one inquire, Mr. Slade, what are
your tastes?" said Mrs. Connop.

An amused smile played about Gilbert's
mouth as he rejoined, "That is a question
that can be answered from so many different

points of view. Professionally, I should
reply, military glory; diplomatically, that
they are those of the lady I am talking to.
Honestly, I should say, catholic in the extreme, as far as I know myself. I should
say I have a keen appreciation of the best
of everything there is going, whether it is
hunting, shooting, travelling, sight-seeing,
or whether it takes the baser form of mere
eating and drinking."

"Ah! Mr. Slade," rejoined Lettie, laughing, "I have some remembrance of that
latter characteristic. I believe he was
starving, auntie, when father found him at
Lincoln."

"Quite true, Miss Devereux. And I can
never be sufficiently thankful that he did
find us. Jocelyn and I were almost capable
of devouring each other."

A peal on the knocker here heralded the
arrival of Mrs. Kynaston, and in another
minute that lady had glided into the room,
shaken hands affectionately with Lettie,

been presented to Mrs. Connop, and exchanged a cordial greeting with Gilbert Slade.

"Glad to catch you at last, Lettie, though
you're one of the latest swallows that ever
made a season. There's nothing new, there
never is, you know, to an old Londoner like
me; they may call it this, they may call it
that, but it is always the old show dished
up under a new name. However, it's all
very pleasant, and I am enjoying myself as
much as ever, and so will you. I heard by
the purest accident in the Park this morning
that you were at the Ramsbury's 'garden'
yesterday. I don't know them myself, but
have always understood they do the thing
prettily."

"Yes, indeed," rejoined Mrs. Connop. "I
don't care where it is, I think there are
very few garden-parties given in London
where you will find the thing better done
than it is at Chelsea."

"Did you happen to be there, Mr. Slade?"
inquired Mrs. Kynaston, carelessly.

"Yes," replied Gilbert, "it was there I discovered Miss Devereux; and it is to that I owe the pleasure of meeting you again."

"Very nice of you to say so," replied Mrs. Kynaston; "and I shall only be too glad, as will my husband, if you can find time to honour us with a call in Chester Street. How is Charlie, Lettie? has he done with Cambridge yet?"

Miss Devereux was slightly discomposed by this question. She detected a defiant sniff on the part of her aunt at once. She knew perfectly well that Mrs. Connop was already fuming because that erratic young gentleman had not paid his *devoirs* in Onslow Gardens. She had particularly requested Gilbert to avoid alluding to him, and now Kate Kynaston had brought his name prominently forward.

"No," she replied, "I have not heard of him lately, but I believe he is still at Cambridge."

"Do you, Lettie?" said Mrs. Connop,

sharply. " I feel pretty sure that he is at the present moment in London."

" You can't be sure, auntie," rejoined Miss Devereux; " in such a city as this, I should think your double, or your treble, for the matter of that, might be about. It is so easy to make a mistake of that kind."

" Ah ! " said Mrs. Kynaston, with some languid curiosity, " you think Mr. Devereux is in town, apparently, Mrs. Connop ? "

" I don't think it, I know he is ; and it's very rude of him not to call."

" Now, Mr. Slade," cried Lettie, " I appeal to you : don't you think it is very possible to make a mistake in the street, and fancy you've seen a person who is not within miles of London ? "

" Certainly," rejoined Gilbert; " as a brother officer of mine remarked on this point, ' Fellahs are so confoundedly alike, you know, there is no knowing them apart ; if they were only like horses, you know, dash it all, you couldn't make a mistake about 'em then.' ''

Mrs. Kynaston inwardly congratulated herself that she had been reticent of speech. It was in perfectly good faith that she had asked if he had done with Cambridge, as she knew that his time there was drawing to a close; but she certainly knew, further, that he had dined with her husband the previous night. That Charlie should be in London and his own sister not know of it puzzled her a little; but Mrs. Kynaston was not the woman to make mischief, and therefore passed Lettie's remark over in silence.

" Come and lunch with me to-morrow," she said, " all of you; and if your brother's shadow should take material form I shall only be too pleased, Lettie, if you will bring him with you. We can have a real good talk then, and I shall be enabled to honestly make your acquaintance, Mrs. Connop. This afternoon I have half-a-dozen places

to go to, and have only time to shake hands
and say how very pleased I shall be to see
you again."

Mrs. Kynaston's invitation was gladly
accepted; even Gilbert Slade thought luncheon with the sparkling, bonny brunette
would be pleasant, and, as before said, he
had an epicurean admiration for pretty
women—though at the present moment he
was regarding these two living, breathing
models much as a man might regard a
couple of pictures—still, they were pleasant
to the eye, and afforded him that gratification that arrives to all of us from the
contemplation of the beautiful. They were
a striking contrast, but both very perfect
in their way. Kate Kynaston's ebon locks,
flashing dark eyes, and well-rounded form,
was a pretty foil to the lithe figure, dark
chestnut tresses, and laughing brown eyes
of her friend.

Mrs. Kynaston could not be said to
puzzle her head much, but she did wonder

a little what had brought Charlie Devereux to town in this somewhat mysterious way. She reflected, also, that her husband was not the man to throw dinners away, and that from those upon whom he bestowed his hospitality he was not so much apt to expect, but to feel certain, of receiving some return. What his object might be in entertaining Mr. Devereux she could not fathom; and she was still further bewildered as to what had led him to entertain Mr. Furzedon. About the latter Mrs. Kynaston had her own opinion; she might be somewhat of a Bohemian, but she had mingled too much with the best people not to know "good form" when she saw it, and her instinct told her that Furzedon was not quite a gentleman. He might pass as such with most men, but a well-bred woman would be sure to detect the base ring in the metal.

Still, that was no business of hers. The Major, as a rule, was a good husband in one respect. Considering in how many others he failed to deserve this definition, it was well that he should have something to the credit side of the ledger. He had scores of dubious acquaintances—men at whom society was wont to look somewhat askance, men of whom, to put it mildly, there were divers queer stories afloat—but, to do him justice, he rarely asked these across his own threshold, nor was Mrs. Kynaston ever thrust into the slightest acquaintance with them. When it was absolutely necessary to his plans that such should make their objectionable appearance, they were relegated strictly to the Major's own den, and his wife knew no more than that "somebody on business" was closeted with him.

How very often invitations are either given or accepted which, on reflection, people feel to have been a great mistake, and Mrs. Kynaston's luncheon invitation had not long left her lips before she became conscious that this was not exactly what she wanted. There was no disguise about her being quite willing to entertain them all, but it suddenly occurred to her that she did not want to entertain them all at the same time, that to have a good gossip with Lettie she wanted that young lady all to herself! That a *téte-à-téte* with Gilbert Slade would be no doubt enjoyable, but would rather lose its flavour with Mrs. Connop and Miss Devereux being there to assist at it. There was nothing mean about Mrs. Kynaston. She was free-handed as an Arab in the matter of hospitality; her impromptu "little lunches" were usually successes, but on this occasion she felt that she had not picked her guests with her usual good judgment. However, she was too much a woman of the world to be disconcerted for a moment about a trifle like this. To recollect a previous engagement, which must necessitate the postponement of their contemplated banquet, was easy, and it was with many apologies to Mrs.

Connop for having spoken so carelessly that
Mrs. Kynaston took her departure. "It
was very stupid of me, but really in the
season no one should speak without looking
at their engagement slate, and she really
had quite forgotten all about that water-
party at the Fitzgeralds. I only wish,
Lettie, they had too, but I've promised
Mrs. Fitzgerald, and, as she has about the
longest and bitterest tongue in all London,
I daren't offend her. I don't know what
crimes might not be laid at my door should
I fail to put in an appearance. A line to
the Thermopolium will, of course, always
find you, Mr. Slade, and you must come
and see me before you wend your way
northwards. For the present, good-bye to
all of you." And then Mrs. Kynaston took
her departure.

Gilbert soon followed her example, and
had hardly left the house when Mrs. Connop
exclaimed, with a snap that made Lettie
start, " Now, what did she mean by that ? "

" Mean ! Who ? What are you thinking of, auntie ? "

" Mrs. Kynaston ! Why did she suddenly withdraw her invitation to lunch ? Don't look so bewildered, child," continued Mrs. Connop, merrily. " It does not much matter, but I have mixed too much in the world not to know that to say one thing and mean another is by no means the exclusive privilege of politicians. The Fitzgeralds' water-party ! Rubbish ! Doubtful whether there are any Fitzgeralds; bet any one Mrs. Kynaston is not going to them to-morrow. She's a very glib liar, Lettie; quite good enough to deceive any man, and most women; but I'm a solicitor's widow, my dear, and exceptionally gifted in the detection of false speech."

" Absurd, auntie ! You are too suspicious. Kate is as liberal a soul as ever lived, and little likely to be niggard of her wine or her cutlets."

" Nonsense ! It's not that I mean. I

have never seen Mrs. Kynaston before, but she changed her mind about having us to lunch. I feel quite sure of it. It is of no consequence, but I am curious about 'the why.'"

"You are prejudiced against Mrs. Kynaston," said Lettie.

"No, my dear, I am not; but it is no use pretending one does not take fancies or aversions at first sight. Dogs, acting up to the lights of their nature, often fight in real earnest on first meeting. Reason tells me I know nothing of Mrs. Kynaston. Instinct tells me to mistrust her."

"Oh, auntie! She is one of my greatest friends," cried Miss Devereux.

"I trust I am wrong, and that you may never rue it. She's a very pretty, pleasant, lady-like woman, but for all that —— Well!

The reason why I cannot tell,
I do not like thee, Dr. Fell.

Say no more, child; but I don't take to Mrs. Kynaston."

CHAPTER XI.

A WAIF ON LIFE'S STREAM.

Let Dick Kynaston's habitation be where it might, one thing was always an imperative necessity. Most men affect more or less to have a sanctum of their own, but with Kynaston it was a *bonâ fide* den, into which even the housemaid was jealously admitted. It was furnished after the Major's own peculiar fancy, and tobacco and the Racing Calendar were predominant features in its arrangement. There the owner, seated at his writing-table, cigar in mouth, would pore for hours over volumes of the great Turf lexicon, and make astounding calculations about weights, distances, and the varied running of horses. He was as great a votary of racing as Norman Slade; if he had not studied so long, he had studied it quite as attentively; but there was this great difference between the two men: whereas the one loved it purely as a sport, and exulted in seeing a good horse win, the other regarded it much as one might the tables at Monaco; he looked upon it as a mere means of gambling, and would infinitely sooner have seen the good horse beaten, had it profited him more. It is curious how this greed for money so constantly is, on the Turf, the cause of its pursuer's undoing. Is not the legend still extant of that luckless book-maker who, after months of infinite patience and manipulation, had succeeded in getting his horse into the Chester Cup at a weight that made it a gift to him. Carefully was the commission worked, and he succeeded in plotting a *coup* that should have made him and his associates rich men for their lives. In a reckless moment, only a few days before the event was to come off, in his anxiety to let no money escape him, he laid the odds to lose ten thousand pounds against a horse, the owner of which had no intention up to that time of sending it to the banks of the Dee. Strange fatality! That very horse upset the deep-laid scheme by a neck, and turned the well-nigh mighty triumph into bitter defeat and disaster.

It was very rarely that any of Dick Kynaston's friends were made welcome to what was conventionally called "the study." Nor was it exactly the room in which a man would elect to receive any one but an extreme intimate. In Chester Street this sanctuary was simply the back dining-room, and, after the books and cigar-boxes, the chief characteristics were a leathern arm-chair and a large, plain, substantial writing-table.

The Major had no connection whatever with literature, but he was certainly a man with very extensive correspondence. The

letters he received and the replies thereto
were generally of the briefest, and a great
many of them were apparently from people
to whom the handling of a pen was a strange
or ? toilsome labour. Their spelling, like their
caligraphy, was of a doubtful order. There
was much uncertainty apparently amongst
them as to the orthodox way of spelling
"Major," and they discovered more varieties
on that point than one would think so simple
a title was capable of. These correspon-
dents not uncommonly followed their letters.
Quiet, unassuming people, as a rule; whose
dress might prompt a well-drilled servitor
to keep his eye on the umbrellas in the
hall, but who otherwise were unmistakeably
business visitors; and they were a strange
and curious lot, these jackals of the Major's.

It was a sad revelation of how educated
men who have sunk beneath life's stormy
waters are driven to get their living, to find
that amongst this little band several of them
were men well educated, and who once held

a good position; ruined mostly by their own mad folly, they had descended to the depths of racecourse touts, or still more often had become the tools of the professional usurers, who in former days had helped them to their ruin. The Major himself, very indignant though he would have been had anyone ventured to hint so, was simply one of these latter in a very large way of business. If he had burnt his fingers considerably, he had not come to utter financial grief. He had never forfeited membership of his clubs, he still held his own very fairly socially, and it was essential to his scheme of life that Mrs. Kynaston should take her place in the world, and be seen where that world of some ten thousand people do please to congregate. The difference between him and his *employés* is obvious. To the well-dressed denizens of Clubland the spendthrift of family and expectations was easily accessible, which, of course, he was not to those more ragged of his brethren long since cast out from the gay scenes of their undoing. What hardly-pressed young man would not welcome the prosperous gentleman in broadcloth and clean linen, who sympathised with his embarrassments over a cigar, and wound up by saying, " Deuce of a mistake, borrowing. But, Lord! what's the use of preaching! Young blood will run its course. I never argue with a man who *must* have money, unless he is trying to demonstrate the possibility of having it out of me. I'll give you a line to old Moggs, if you like. He'll rob you, naturally—they all do. It's their trade, but he'll let you have it as cheap as any man in London."

Amongst Dick Kynaston's habitual visitors was that luckless individual who has already twice flitted across the pages of this narrative. We have seen him righteously struck to the earth by Furzedon outside the nighthouse in the Haymarket. Unjustifiable though the provocation was,

it was questionable whether the striker
should not have refrained from that blow.
We have met him again as a mere race-
course tout at Lincoln Races, speaking in
the slang vernacular of his tribe, and yet
Prance was a man of good education, who
had known a much better position, and
who, though some years older than Ralph
Furzedon, had been tempted by that pre-
cocious young gentleman to his undoing.
How that happened will appear later; for
the present it suffices to say that to Dick
Kynaston he is a mere purveyor of racing
intelligence, picked up it is impossible to
say how, but at all times worth listening to,
as the Major has discovered from experience.
That there had ever been the slightest connection between Furzedon and Mr. Prance,
Kynaston was totally unaware. Had he
been a spectator of that scene in the Haymarket no one would have been keener to
know what called forth the final malediction
launched against Ralph Furzedon, and what

had been the previous relations between the
pair to warrant the bitter intensity in which
it was couched. The ordinary rough, who,
in his avocation of robbery, gets knocked
down, may swear a little, but takes it
usually after the manner of his betters, as a
mishap in the matter of business; but, as
we know, the casual lookers-on had felt that
no ordinary discomfiture in a street row
could have brought forth the animosity con-
centrated in Mr. Prance's curse.

It is the morning after the Major's little
dinner at the Thermopolium that, while
engaged in those mystic calculations somewhat akin to the researches of the old
alchemists in their untiring, though un-
availing, endeavours to transmute baser
metals into gold, the Major was informed
that "a person" wanted to see him. Like
the old alchemists, Kynaston had discovered
that much more human but baser secret,
that it is quite possible to induce the weaker
portion of humanity to part with their small

store of wealth with a view to increasing it.
Now, " a person to see you " is an announcement disturbing to a considerable portion of
society generally. The " person to see you "
is apt to be a very undesirable person to
interview—apt to either want money in
some form, or be the bearer of disagreeable
intelligence. We all know it except those
affluent past redemption, and for whom some
special paradise of their own must be pre-
served, or those, and they are a very limited
number, whose record is so entirely blame-
less that they can laugh at the idea of the
limelight being turned upon it. But the
Major was used to this curt announcement.
He neither dreaded that Miss Minnever
had called to say that unless she had one
hundred on Mrs. Kynaston's account she
should be compelled to take legal proceedings; nor had he any fear of similar threats
from creditors on his own account. Dick
Kynaston was a business man in this wise :
whatever he might have done once, he was

a pretty rigidly ready-money man now. He made his wife a fairly liberal allowance, but he had given her pretty sharply to understand that this must never be exceeded. Therefore this announcement brought no misgivings to his mind.

Another minute, and the servant had ushered into his room Mr. Prance.

"Well," said the Major, "what is it? Sit down, and don't let us waste any time about it. We know one another pretty well now. If you merely want money, say so. You know I'm usually good for a trifle, and I will tell you at once what I can let you have. If you've brought me information, you know very well that you can trust me to pay for it, if I find it valuable."

" Well, Major," replied Prance, as he seated himself in a chair, " I've brought you a bit of Turf information which, I think, is worth your taking note of. I can't say it's valuable, probably never may be. You're a business man, and I don't

expect you'll ever think you owe me anything on that account. But I've got something else to say to you. I believe you
were hunting up in the wolds of Lincolnshire last year. Didn't you make the acquaintance of a Mr. Devereux? We both
saw him ride at Lincoln, and, mind you, he
will ride some day, but he's got to prac-
tise a bit yet. Now, I've heard something
about that young gentleman. He's got into
trouble a bit, and, from the little that I can
learn, is falling into about the worst hands
that could happen to any young man start-
ing in life."

It took a good deal to astonish the Major,
but that Prance should be aware that he
was mixed up in Charlie Devereux's affairs
did surprise him. He hesitated a little before he made answer. It was scarcely likely
that a man like Prance would presume to
come and tell him to his face that he was
no fit mentor for youth. Prance, with a
direct pecuniary interest in keeping on good

terms with him, was hardly likely to commit himself in this fashion. What did he mean? What did he know? What could the fellow be driving at?

"Yes," replied the Major, slowly, "I know Mr. Charles Devereux and all his people, but I am not aware that he has fallen into particularly bad hands."

"Did you ever come across a man of the name of Furzedon?" said Prance, lowering his voice.

"I know a *gentleman* of that name," replied Kynaston, as he rose from his chair and assumed a lounging attitude against the mantelpiece.

"*Gentleman!*" retorted the other with a bitter sneer. "You may call him that if you like. There's a good many travel under that name who, if it means anything like straightforwardness and honesty, have little right to it. From the little I've seen, but more from what I've heard, I believe that

Furzedon is a great friend of Mr. Devereux's."

"Mr. Furzedon, you mean," observed the Major, quietly.

"No, sir, I don't," rejoined Prance, doggedly. "I'll call him 'that Furzedon.' But if you're a friend of Mr. Devereux's tell him to take care of himself, for that he's intimate with as slippery a young scoundrel as ever trod the Heath at Newmarket."

"Surely, Mr. Furzedon does very little in that way?"

"Look here, Major," said his visitor, "you go about a good deal, and are supposed to have cut your eye-teeth, just judge for yourself. Another hint, and it's worth a sovereign, too. I don't know what sort of a card-player you are, but, if ever you take a hand with Furzedon, don't be too sure of getting the best of it."

"Ah!" rejoined the Major, "I don't suppose that is very likely to happen, but it *is* worth a trifle to know that your antagonist is of the highest class when you sit down. Now you recollect what I asked you to find out if possible. Have you succeeded?"

" I don't know that I can quite say that," replied Prance, diffidently, "and I shall have to write to you again on the subject, still, as far as I can make out, they have got no first-class two-year-old in the Northern stables."

"All right!" replied the Major, as he handed the tout a gratuity. "If you discover one later on, you must let me know. And now, good-bye," and a curt nod of dismissal indicated to Mr. Prance that his audience was terminated.

"Ah!" said the Major to himself, after his visitor had left the room, " I was somewhat deceived in that young man. I did not think him a fool, but I had no idea he was so precociously clever. I must study him a bit. I wonder how much he has had to say to young Devereux's losses? I shouldn't wonder if my friend Prance knows an ugly story or two about him, the possession of which would render him very amenable to reason if he and I should ever happen to differ? And it's a quarrelsome world," mused the Major, "and men lose their temper as often as they do their money, and sometimes, sad to say, both simultaneously." Mr. Prance's hint was quite a revelation to the Major. He had regarded Furzedon as a quiet, tolerably well-mannered young man, not at all likely to exhibit speculative tastes, but, according to this informant, Mr. Furzedon was an exceedingly astute young one, with a decided taste for gambling in every form. Dick Kynaston had been brought up too much amongst "the right people" not to detect that there was a dash of Brummagem about Ralph Furzedon. He was a very good imitation, but the initiated could not fail to see that he was not quite genuine. The base coin appears good money to the eye, but it won't ring, it jars upon the ear when put to that test, and similarly Furzedon, though at first he thoroughly passed muster, when you came to associate with him, jarred a little on the feelings. You couldn't quite indicate the flaw, but you felt intuitively that he was not quite a gentleman.

Suddenly a thought flashed across the Major's mind. A confederate might be useful in many of the transactions in which he was habitually engaged, especially a confederate over whom he had a hold. And this he thought, through Prance, very possible in the case of Ralph Furzedon. There was plenty of time to make inquiries, for he had no particular scheme on foot at the present moment that required a coadjutor. The Major then seated himself at his writing-table, and made some brief and mysterious memoranda in his betting-book, without which volume, unless perchance it had been in his bath, Dick Kynaston had for years never been met with.

CHAPTER XII.

BOB BRADDOCK'S CONDITIONS.

"So I'm to be civil to Mr. Furzedon, am
I?" mused Mrs. Kynaston, as she sat in her
pretty drawing-room the day after her meeting with Miss Devereux. " Now I wonder
what that means. Dick never gives me
those instructions without a reason. I don't
particularly fancy Mr. Furzedon myself; I
wonder what Lettie thinks of him. She had
ample opportunity of studying him during
the month he was at North Leach; however, as she is coming to lunch here, I shall
have an opportunity of ascertaining."

Miss Devereux was true to her appointment, and the two ladies sat down to their

meal *tête-à-tête*. After gossiping gaily over varigus subjects, Lettie asked her friend whether she thought there was any chance of their taking The Firs again next winter.

"I am sure I can't say," replied Mrs. Kynaston. "You see men like my husband now and then don't hunt at all. Dick will race, and there are bad years as well as good ones at that amusement; and then we can't afford horses. The Firs is a cheap place, but I don't think Dick quite liked it. He prefers a more thickly populated neighbourhood. By-the-way, have you seen anything of that Mr. Furzedon who was staying with you last winter?"

"Oh, yes; he called the other day. He has quite done with Cambridge, you know, now, and is settled in London."

"Yes," replied Kate, "I have an idea he is trying hard to push his way into London society. What did you think of him, Lettie?"

"He made himself very pleasant while he

was with us—was very good-natured, and
seemed to enjoy himself."

"All of which, my dear," said Mrs. Kynaston, laughing, "does not give me the
slightest insight into what you think of him.
Do you consider him quite good form? Is
he of the same stamp as Mr. Slade, for instance?"

"No," rejoined Miss Devereux, quickly;
"but he is a soldier, and there is something
different about soldiers, you know. I am
so anxious that Charlie should become one.
He is much too fond of hunting to become
a clergyman, and I'm sure he would never
do any good as a barrister, and he must be
something."

"Quite so," replied Mrs. Kynaston, with
mock gravity; "men must be something, if it
is only to keep them out of mischief, and
they don't always do that. Charlie would
make a very dashing hussar; and I ought to be
a judge, for I knew the ringing of bits and
bridles well in my early married days. Dick

didn't sell out for a couple of years after we married. Mr. Slade *is* good-looking," she continued, after a momentary pause. "Don't you think so?"

"Yes," rejoined Lettie; "it is one of those dark, handsome faces we are all apt to go wild about."

"He can be very agreeable too when he likes. I hope you found him so the other day at Lady Ramsbury's."

"Very much so," replied Miss Devereux. "I am glad to say that there is a chance of seeing a little of him next winter."

"How so?" inquired Mrs. Kynaston.

"His regiment has been moved up to York, and the dragoons from there often come down to our county balls; besides, he has declared that he will come down and see Polestar run at Lincoln in the autumn."

Mrs. Kynaston cast one quick look at her companion, and wondered how far she and Mr. Slade were interested in each other. Kate Kynaston felt almost inclined to resent this idea. She had commenced a slight flirtation with Gilbert at Lincoln; and when Mrs. Kynaston did that she was wont to regard a man as her own peculiar property, and looked for unswerving allegiance on his part Like many women of her type, she was very good-tempered and pleasant till you happened to interfere with any of her schemes or caprices; and then one who should have known her well—for had he not been in the toils?—said,

"You may look out for squalls; you've got one of the cleverest women in England against you, and it's long odds she carries her point, more especially if she is playing against a man."

Gilbert Slade is lounging in the smoking-room of the Thermopolium with a view to, if possible, catching hold of Major Braddock. He had promised to consult his uncle as to whether he could assist young Devereux to a nomination for the army, a fact which, when it came to Mrs. Kynaston's ears, disconcerted that lady not a little. She argued that when men exerted themselves to assist young ladies' brothers, they, at all events, have considerable admiration for the young lady herself; and Mrs. Kynaston, upon very insufficient grounds, considered that Gilbert had no business just at present to admire anybody but Kate Kynaston. She need not have perturbed herself, that *insouciant* hussar thought of his two recent acquaintances only as a couple of pretty, agreeable women; but he certainly did go this length, that of the two he preferred Miss Devereux. No very great preference, perhaps, but still such it was as far as it went. It would have angered both ladies to know that what occupied his mind at the present moment much more than their fair selves was the nuisance of having to go back to York. York was all very well when you came to the grouse-time, the races, and the hunting; but York during the London season was unendurable. He loathed the loud blare of the barrack-yard; he knew how hot and dusty Coney Street would be; everybody would be away, and an evening country ride without any object was not much for a man to look forward to. "No wonder," he muttered, "we soldiers drink a good deal of claret, and rather stiffen our points at whist in these dull country quarters. What a deuce of a bore it is having to go back."

When his uncle entered the smoking-room he at once confided his grievances to him; but that veteran simply "d——d his impudence," and called him a discontented young dog. "By Jove, sir," he said, "it would do you a lot of good to get a good rattling Irish out-station. I had one once myself. My troop was detached from Dun-dalk; there wasn't a soul to speak to, and as for dining, I didn't do such a thing for four months;" and the Major quite shuddered at the hardships he had undergone upon that occasion.

"It's a wonder you ever pulled through," said Gilbert laughing.

"I don't know that I should have done so," replied his uncle, twinkling his eye, "if I hadn't made friends with the priest. He had some marvellous whisky, and was the only man I ever met who could really brew whisky-punch. By Jove, sir, I lived upon it. He taught me to play 'spoiled five,' and I'd just get through the evening that way till the cards began to get hazy, and I felt it was time to go home. It's a beautiful game, spoiled five; but his reverence used to take the sixpences out of me amazingly; I dare say he played a better game, but I know he had a better head for punch."

"You think he rather rooked you, then?" said Gilbert.

"Pooh, nonsense! we played for merely nominal stakes; but Father O'Shea was a keen card-player, and, like Mrs. Battle, loved the rigour of the game. I was generally foggy towards the end of the proceedings."

" I say, uncle," said Gilbert quietly, " you've lots of interest, you know, at the Horse Guards ; do you think you could get a nomination for a commission for a young fellow in whom I am interested ?"

" Young fellow in whom you are interested ! friend of yours, I presume ?"

" Well, I can't exactly say that," rejoined Slade ; " for the fact is I barely know him."

"Then what the deuce do you mean?" rejoined the Major; " you can't expect me to go bothering at the Horse Guards to ask favours for your slight acquaintances."

" Well," rejoined the hussar, coolly, " his sister is a deuced nice girl, and I've promised to do what I can to help her in this matter."

Major Braddock's sole reply was a low chuckle, and an expressive wink. The suspicion of a sentimental affair was apt to arouse the mirth of that *bon vivant*, who believed in nothing but sensual gratification.

"I say, Bertie, my boy, spoons at your time of life is only natural. You will find out the vanity of it before you're much older. Only, as far as my authority goes, and remember you'll have most of my dollars when I go, I bar matrimony before you've got your troop. If you don't think you are better as a bachelor, then, please yourself. I've nothing more to say against it."

"Your warning is quite uncalled for," rejoined Gilbert Slade. "One may like and admire a girl without the slightest thought of marrying her. Besides, I am quite of your opinion. It ought to be made illegal for subalterns to marry. But will you help me in this matter?"

"I can't say. You admit you know nothing about this young fellow. I've no doubt his sister is a nice, ladylike girl.

You are not likely to make a mistake about that. But the prettiest and nicest of them are sometimes cursed with the most objectionable brothers."

" I can assure you young Devereux will pass muster."

" Not a bit of use, Master Bertie. I'll not go begging till I have seen him. I've too great a regard for Her Majesty's service to inflict upon any regiment a youngster whom his brother officers might feel ought never to have been amongst them. Let me see him, and then, if I conscientiously can, I'll do my best for him."

" I am afraid there will be some little difficulty about that," said Bertie, meditatively.

" I can't help it," replied the Major, testily. " I have told you I won't back a dark horse. You surely can't be afraid to show him, because that's enough to d—— him at once."

" Nonsense, uncle Robert; it's not that. The slight difficulty is this: That he is at the present moment at Cambridge, and I don't know whether he can get away; while at the same time my leave is running out, and I must return to York. Of course I can say nothing until I have seen Miss Devereux; but I don't quite see my way into bringing you together before the end of the season. And when I am in town in the winter you are as likely as not to be staying at some country house or another."

"Can't be helped, Bertie," returned the Major, doggedly; "as I said before, I'll see him before I back him. How it is to be managed is your business; but if you ask us to meet at dinner, for goodness sake, my dear boy, let me run my eye over the *menu*. Boys of your age never understand eating.

'Man may live without love—what is passion but pining?
But where is the man who can live without dining?'"

There was no more poetry in the Major than in an oyster, and I question much whether he knew anything about " Owen

Meredith's " poem as a whole, but that one passage he certainly had by heart, he thoroughly endorsed every line of it, and was rather given to quoting it.

Gilbert felt there was no more to be said. His uncle had delivered his ultimatum, and the bringing of Charlie and Major Braddock together he felt could only be compassed after consultation with Miss Devereux. He nodded to his uncle as the latter left the room, and continued to smoke on in silent meditation. He had, at all events, success-fully accomplished the first step. He had no fear but what Charlie Devereux would pass muster with the Major, and the veteran had given his word to interest himself in his behalf should that be the case.

It must be remembered that the days of which I am writing were before the time of competition, when a nomination for a regi-ment held good, providing you passed a certain specified examination, a more prac-tical test to my mind than the present

system, which is calculated to furnish the
army with excellent linguists and arith-
meticians, but not quite the best stuff from
which soldiers are made. I am afraid this
higher knowledge is of little account in the
field, however telling it may be in the class-
room. There was a hero who won the V.C.
scarce a decade ago, whom rumour declared
had been twice "plucked" in one of the
ceaseless examinations that now dog the
steps of the unfortunate British officer, but
he had great determination, quickness, and
grit, which served him in better stead that
day than science or the gift of tongues.

The one thing quite clear to Gilbert Slade
is that he must see Miss Devereux without
loss of time, and accordingly, as soon as it
became near the canonical hour for calling,
he wended his way towards Onslow Gardens.
He arrived there somewhat early, but he
did this with intention, as he honestly
wanted to get in. To his inquiry as to
whether Mrs. Connop was at home, he re-

ceived an answer in the affirmative, and was duly ushered upstairs. To his dismay he found that estimable lady alone, and after the warning he had received the other day from Miss Devereux he knew that it would be imprudent to ask her for her nephew's address. However, there could be no harm in asking after Lettie, and his mind was considerably lightened when he ascertained that that young lady was not only in, but would probably be down in a few minutes.

"She is just putting on her bonnet, Mr. Slade, as we are going over to Lady Ramsbury's for a cup of tea, and intend to have a turn in the Park afterwards."

A few minutes' lively conversation, for Mrs. Connop was by no means one of those women whom talking to becomes painful and wearisome labour, and then Lettie entered the room, looking, as Slade thought, handsomer than he had ever seen her yet. She greeted Gilbert with much cordiality,

and then, to Slade's great relief, Mrs. Connop
got up, and said, laughingly :

"I must leave you to take care of Mr.
Slade, Lettie. I am sure you will excuse
me for a few minutes," she added, turning
to Gilbert, "but I also must array myself
for our drive."

"I wanted much to see you alone for a
few minutes, Miss Devereux," said Gilbert,
as the door closed. "I have lost no time
in seeing if I could be of any assistance to
your brother in obtaining a commission.
Now, my uncle, popularly known as 'Jolly
Bob Braddock,' can, as I told you, help him,
if he chooses, and he has promised he will if
he likes him."

"Likes him!" repeated Lettie. "But
that is rather a doubtful thing."

"You don't know the Major, and therefore you can't quite understand. He is
straight as a die, but he won't exert his
influence to procure a commission for any
young fellow whom he does not consider

pleasant and a gentleman—in short, he insists upon seeing him."

"Oh dear!" exclaimed Lettie, with a comic expression of despair, "this is terrible. It's worse than going in for his 'smalls.'"

"Nothing of the kind," replied Gilbert. "There will be no trouble about it if I can only get hold of your brother at once, and induce him to meet my uncle at the Thermopolium. As long as his dinner is all right —and, as we have agreed that he is to have the ordering of it, it will be hard lines if it isn't—Charlie will pass muster triumphantly, and, I hope, spend a pleasant evening. But, you see, my time in London is limited, and the question is, Can he get away from Cambridge?"

"He *is* away, Mr. Slade; I believe him to be in London at this minute, though I don't know his address; but I think it very possible I may in the course of the day. I have written to a great friend of his, who is

pretty certain to know where he is staying,
and I will let you know the moment I hear.
He is very keen upon this army idea, and, I
am sure, would make a great effort in answer
to your kindness; and it really is very kind
of you, Mr. Slade, to have taken so much
trouble for people of whom you know so
little as you do of us."

"That is a fault to be amended, Miss
Devereux," rejoined Gilbert. "You cast
your bread upon the waters that bitter afternoon at Lincoln, and won undying gratitude
from a half-famished man."

"It is very good of you to make so little
of the service you are rendering us." And,
as Lettie spoke, the door opened, and Mrs.
Connop sailed into the room.

Gilbert felt that his mission was accomplished, and, though he would willingly have
prolonged his *tête-à-tête*, there was nothing
left him now but to put the ladies into their
carriage and take his departure.

CHAPTER XIII.

SEEKING A COMMISSION.

Mr. Furzedon was a little puzzled on the receipt of Miss Devereux's note. There was no difficulty about giving Charlie's address, but it was just possible that young gentleman, for the day or two he was in town, might not care about seeing his relations. What had brought him up Furzedon did not know; he had had no opportunity of private conversation with him at Dick Kynaston's dinner, but he did know that unless the University had intimated they could dispense with Mr. Devereux's presence for some time or even altogether, that his stay in London must be very short. However, after a few minutes' consideration, it was obvious to him that the best thing to do would be to consult Charlie himself on that point. That young gentleman, as soon as he had read the note, observed, "All right, I didn't mean going to Onslow Gardens, but Lettie is a clear-headed girl, and wouldn't particularly want to see me unless she had good reason for it. I had no idea my respected aunt knew I was in town, or else I should have gone up there yesterday. Mrs. Connop has a great idea as to what is due to her from her nephews and nieces, and, as she is a regular trump, I wouldn't offend her for the world."

" You'd be a precious fool if you did," rejoined Furzedon. " She's good, no doubt, for many years to come, but she has money to leave behind her whenever she makes an end of it."

" I wasn't thinking of that," rejoined Charlie curtly. " I only remembered she was always a jolly kind aunt to me from my schoolboy days, when she used to take me to the pantomime, till last winter, when she gave me a cheque for fifty pounds to buy another hunter with."

" I see," replied Furzedon, " one of those beneficent godmamas that only exist in fairy tales. This is the first I ever heard of in real life."

" Perhaps not. I fancy aunt Connop is a sort you don't often come across."

"Well, good morning," rejoined Furzedon. " I shall write a line to Miss Devereux to say that you'll be in Onslow Gardens this afternoon. An independent aunt who is lavish of cheques for fifty is a relative to cling to, take my word for it."

Charlie's appearance in Onslow Gardens that afternoon speedily made his peace with Mrs. Connop. With that lady, indeed, he was an especial favourite. She liked him better considerably than his steady-going brother, and, though very fond of Lettie, perhaps cared more about the scapegrace of the family than her niece. Charlie had never done anything very terrible, but he had a knack—some men have—of being incessantly in scrapes. He had never come actually to grief, but from his earliest days he had occasioned considerable anxiety to his family by perpetually hovering on the brink of it. Lettie was his most trusted counsellor, and in small financial muddles, at her instigation, Mrs. Connop had more than once come to the rescue. Clear-headed Lettie saw, that, with a nature like her brother's, the sooner he was set to some serious work the better. She knew he was doing no good at the University, and she was now very hot upon his getting into the army as soon as possible. You can't keep a man in leading-strings, but to let him saunter through life with no occupation is bad for any, destruction to some.

The preliminary greetings over, Lettie plunged at once *in medias res*, and had the satisfaction of finding both her auditors thoroughly with her. Mrs. Connop was as keen that Charlie should enter the army as he was to get into it, and said that, to see her nephew a dragoon, she would not at all grudge contributing handsomely towards his outfit. And then Lettie went on to tell Charlie how she had persuaded Mr. Slade to ask his uncle, Major Braddock, to interest himself in his— Charlie's—favour, and how that distinguished officer had promised to do so, providing that he approved of this candidate for military honours.

" But, Charlie, Major Braddock will see you—to use Mr. Slade's words, he won't recommend a recruit he hasn't himself inspected; but Mr. Slade says—and it's awfully kind of him—that, if you could manage to dine with him at the Thermopolium one day next week, he will get his uncle to meet you."

" It is very good of him," replied Charlie, " and I will manage it if he will only let me know what day; but remember, I must go back to Cambridge to-night. I have only leave for three days" (he didn't think it necessary to mention that he had obtained leave of absence for three days under pretext of consulting a London physician) ; " but I can always manage to run up and get back by the first train in the morning" And Charlie felt, though he did not venture to express it, that he would willingly risk being sent down, sooner than miss this chance of getting a nomination for a profession he had now set his heart on.

" Very well, then," said Lettie; " I shall write and tell him you will gratefully accept his invitation, if he will forward it to your Cambridge address."

" That's all right," rejoined Charlie gleefully. " And now, aunt, I must say good-bye. You are a trump, Lettie ;" and having given his sister a hearty kiss, and shaken hands with his aunt, Charlie shot down the stairs and made his way back to Duke Street.

Charlie's meditations were a little mixed as he walked westward. He was in high spirits at the idea of the opening which presented itself to him; but the usual bitterness was mingled in the cup, to wit, that he would have to make some arrangements about those confounded bills. Still, his aunt Connop had just distinctly said that she would come down with something handsome to see him a dragoon. Perhaps she would see him out of this scrape. She had done so once or twice before in a small way, but Charlie felt rather afraid of confessing the extent of his misdoings this time to his sister, and she was the medium through which he generally approached his aunt. However, he thought, " Only let me once get into the army, and some of them, I think, are bound to see me through it."

As he passed through Piccadilly Charlie took out his watch, and wondered whether he had time to turn into Chester Street, and call upon Mrs. Kynaston. He was

beginning now to entertain a lively appreciation of that lady's charms. In the hunt-
ing-field she had a serious rival in the
goddess Diana, for the prettiest woman in
England would have had to ride hard and
straight to keep Charlie in her company
while hounds were running, but in London
it was very different. There Mrs. Kynaston
had no rival in Charlie's estimation, and,
miss his train or not, he determined to call.
" Yes, Mrs. Kynaston was at home," so the
servant informed him, and he was duly
ushered into that lady's pretty little drawing-
room in Chester Street.

She received him with much *empressement*, for he really was a favourite of hers,
and was quite aware of his admiration for
herself. She thought sometimes with a
saucy air of triumph of their first meeting,
and how utterly oblivious he had been to
the fact that he was doing escort to a very
pretty woman, and Kate Kynaston would

softly murmur to herself, " Things would be very different now, I think."

" Delighted to see you, Mr. Devereux. Are you up in town for long? Heard you were dining with my husband last night; but I suppose they don't give you a long furlough from Cambridge ?"

" No," laughed Charlie; " very short, indeed, but I hope soon—yes, very soon— to have done with it. I have a chance of entering the army, and if that comes off I shall cut Cambridge at once. Don't you think I shall be right ? "

" Yes, indeed, I do," replied Mrs. Kynaston. " You will make a very fair dragoon, and I don't think you ' frame ' for anything like bookwork."

" That's just what Lettie says," exclaimed Charlie.

" Yes. The life will just suit you—and remember I speak as a woman having experience."

"I don't think I am clever," replied Devereux, laughing; "but you needn't tell a fellow so, Mrs. Kynaston. I think I can ride a bit, and play a decent game of billiards. I had some tough battles with the Major the other night, and had decidedly the best of it."

"Perhaps he was not in form," replied Mrs. Kynaston, drily. "My husband takes a good deal of beating in a general way."

"And I flatter myself I do also," rejoined Charlie, a little piqued. "No, I honestly believe I am a few points better than the Major."

"Well, perhaps, *it* is so," replied Mrs. Kynaston, "only recollect that my husband has had far wider experience than you have had. He is apt to play carelessly except for money."

"We had a trifle on, just to make it interesting," replied Charlie.

"Well, perhaps, you *are* the best," said

Mrs. Kynaston, indifferently, "only I wouldn't be too sure. How is Polestar?"

"Doing wonderfully well, I hear, and very much improved since we got so disgracefully beaten at Lincoln. I hope to avenge my defeat there in the autumn, and that you will be there to see it."

"I hope so too," rejoined Mrs. Kynaston. "But our movements at present are very uncertain. The Major never makes up his mind until the end of the season, and very often not until the end of October."

Major Kynaston's movements were in good truth governed considerably by his financial success on the Turf, as his wife had confided to Lettie, but Mrs. Kynaston was not likely to enter into such confidences with Charlie.

"And when do you expect to go up for your inspection? Lettie told me all about it, and I know that you are to be paraded before Major Braddock. I trust that the wine may be properly iced, and that the cook may have done his *devoirs* deftly," continued Mrs. Kynaston, laughing. " I suppose you know that a mistake in a side-dish, or the claret served at an undue temperature, may nip your aspirations in the bud ? "

" Yes," replied Charlie, joining in her laugh. " I have heard that Major Braddock regards dinner as a very solemn function; but we are to dine at his own club, and surely there should be safety in that. I should think the *chef* for his own sake would do his best for Major Braddock."

" There is much worldly wisdom in your speech," rejoined Mrs. Kynaston. " *Gour-mets* like Major Braddock ' back their bills,' and make bitter the lives of both cook and committee should even their mutton-chop not be done to the exact turn."

" Let us hope the Fates will be propitious. And now, Mrs. Kynaston, I must wish you good-bye, for I have but just time to pack up my traps and catch my train."

" Good-bye, and may all success attend

you. Write as soon as you know; or,
better still, come and tell me you are to be
a dragoon."

Kate Kynaston sat plunged in reverie for
some time after Charlie had taken his departure. She knew her husband too well to
suppose that the light-hearted boy would
have any chance with him at cards or
billiards. What could Dick mean? He
surely did not intend to plunder such small
game as Charlie Devereux, and yet that the
latter had any chance with her husband at
billiards or cards she did not believe for
one moment. Poor Kate! it was far from
her nature to turn hawk, and she had
winced at first when her eyes were opened
to the fact that Dick Kynaston got his
living for the most part by his skill in all
description of "play." But she soon grew
callous, and even stooped to make use of
her own smiles and bright eyes to lure men
into her husband's net. But she was loyal
to her favourites, and Dick, though he ruled

her with an iron hand, on the whole knew
that, now and again she would stand no
plundering of the innocents. It was on
behalf of the young ones Kate chiefly interfered. Her elder admirers, she deemed,
ought to be able to take care of themselves,
but she would interfere sharply sometimes
on behalf of her boyish adorers, and she was
just the sort of woman whom quite young
men especially worship. I don't mean to
say that Kate Kynaston had not plenty of
men of all ages at her feet, but she had a
quiet way with her that put " young ones "
at their ease in the first half-hour. No, she
would not have this thing. She would tell
Dick that he must stay his hand as far as
Charlie Devereux was concerned. She knew
that he was wild, and she knew that he was
weak, but she would not have it on her con-
science that she stood by and saw this boy
ruined on the threshold of his career. She
was submissive in general, and Dick Kynaston was not the man to bear the thwart-

ing of his schemes patiently, but this matter should be speedily settled between them, and she would let him know that Charlie Devereux must be spared.

Then her thoughts ran back to the old channel. She did not deceive herself in the least. She knew that her liking for Gilbert Slade was growing on her. She knew it from the dismay with which she had learnt that he had interfered in Charlie Devereux's behalf at Lettie's request. Gilbert, she argued, must be much struck with that young lady to take all this trouble on her brother's account. She had taken a great fancy to Lettie, but unfortunately she had taken an equally strong one for Slade, and when two such friendships clash it is pretty safe to predict that the woman will be thrown over in favour of the man.

Again, Mrs. Kynaston had chosen, in virtue of her prior acquaintance, to regard Gilbert Slade as her own peculiar property. How very slight that acquaintance had been was shown by the fact that when he met her on old Tom Devereux's drag at Lincoln he had failed to remember her. True, Gilbert had devoted himself to her upon that occasion more than to Lettie, but a man would have laughed at Mrs. Kynaston's entertaining such an idea that she held right of vassalage over Gilbert, though a woman would perfectly have understood it, and have divined in a moment that the friendship of those two would be of short duration now that Mrs. Kynaston's jealousy was aroused. That lady, rousing herself at length from her reverie, sprang to her feet, and, as she paced up and down the drawing-room, was quite as determined that Lettie Devereux should never wed Gilbert Slade as that her husband should not plunder the brother.

CHAPTER XIV.

CHARLIE ON PROBATION.

GILBERT SLADE contrived to see a good deal of Miss Devereux during this last fortnight. As the diplomatist who had the arranging a meeting between Charlie and Major Braddock on the most favourable terms, he found it necessary to consult Lettie very often. The Major usually, and more especially at this time of year, had pretty numerous engagements in the dinner way. Therefore it was necessary to ascertain, first, what evening would suit him. Then it was imperative that Charlie should be written to, and told that if anything should prevent his

attending on that occasion he must tele-
graph at once, as otherwise he would create
a "most unfavourable impression on the
Major, who regarded engagements of this
sort as bonds of the most solemn description.
Charlie also had to be cautioned against the
heinous sin of unpunctuality. Very fond
was the Major of laying down the axiom,
that to be late on such an occasion was an
insult both to your host and his cook.
When in the army he had been always
given to harrying the subalterns about being
late for mess. Unpunctuality on other
parades he might look over, but not on this
one; so that altogether Gilbert was a good
deal in Onslow Gardens. However, at last
everything was arranged. Charlie had been
most carefully tutored, as far as Lettie,
inspired by Slade, could do so by the post.
He had even been tutored into studying
"Lucille," and warned, if he saw a fair
opportunity, to fire off the following quotation from that poem :—

" We may live without friends,
      We may live without books ;
   But civilised men
      Cannot live without cooks."

"I am so very anxious," said Lettie, when the important day was finally fixed. " I do so hope Charlie will acquit himself creditably. I have done as you told me. I have warned him to be highly appreciative of the good things set before him; but to be a little diffident as to giving an opinion about the wine."

" Quite right !" said Gilbert, laughing. "Very young men are apt to set up as judges in that respect, and I know that always moves uncle Bob's wrath. I even once heard him assert that no man knew anything about wine until he had had a fit of the gout."

" But," cried Lettie, " men don't always have the gout, do they?"

" I fancy my uncle and his cronies are unanimous concerning that complaint. We must only hope that he is not disposed to it just now."

"It is very good of you, Mr. Slade, to take all this trouble for me, and I am very grateful to you; but I feel wofully nervous about Charlie's ordeal. Your uncle seems somewhat peculiar."

"Not at all, Miss Devereux; not more so than the generality of mankind. The only thing is, that, as I want Charlie to show to the best advantage, I'm giving you a chart of the country. We have most of us peculiarities, and it is just our clashing of these that makes people take a dislike to us when we first meet them."

"It is very good of you, and I can't be sufficiently grateful."

"Don't think of it," interrupted Gilbert; "I'm only too pleased that I managed to arrange the matter before my time was up. I must leave London the day after to-morrow, and I was so afraid that it might not come off."

"But I shall see you again before you go?" said Lottie.

"Oh, yes, I'll come down to-morrow afternoon, if you'll allow me, and tell you how things went off. And now I must say adieu. Depend on it, it will be all right, Miss Devereux. Uncle Bob is a good-natured fellow, though perhaps over-fond of his dinner, and has always done anything I wanted;" and with these words of encouragement Gilbert Slade took his departure.

Lettie was very anxious that Charlie should get into the army. She had been greatly pleased with the enthusiasm he showed at the prospect, and it was therefore no wonder that she should be anxious about his success.

"It's odd," thought Lettie, "but really at present his chance seems to depend on the caprice of a middle-aged gentleman." Then she thought how very kind Mr. Slade had been about the whole business; and

CHARLIE ON PROBATION.			237

then I think her whole reverie rather con-
centrated itself on Mr. Slade himself. It is
a very easy transition, when the subject is
a good-looking young man, to glide from
" how very kind" to " how very nice " he
was, and from that to those day-dreams in
which all young ladies are prone to indulge,
and to what answer she should give if ever
he should ask the momentous question, and
from that the whole thing dies away in a
background of orange-flowers, bridesmaids,
rice, and old slippers.

The fateful evening at last arrived. Charlie
Devereux, having compared his watch with
the Horse Guards in the afternoon—the one
authority on time that Major Braddock recognised, to which all other clocks were
expected to bend — arrived at the Thermopolium at least ten minutes before the
appointed hour. Gilbert shook him heartily
by the hand, and said, laughing,

" This will do. Uncle Robert is not here
himself yet. Don't forget the hints I have

sent you; I know you'll excuse my doing so, but of course we have a point to carry: appreciative but not demonstrative about the dinner, and somewhat diffident on the subject of wine; bear in mind it's all the Major's ordering; and everything is sure to be good, or else I prophesy a very stormy morrow down below for the cook and butler."

"I shall do my very best," rejoined Charlie, "to profit by your hints. As I am terribly in earnest about this thing, I hope I shall pass muster. Anyway I can't sufficiently thank you, Slade, for the trouble you have taken about it!"

"Nonsense!" replied the other, "but hush, here comes the great pasha himself."

"To the minute, uncle Robert. Let me introduce my friend Mr. Devereux."

The Major shook hands cordially with Charlie, but at the same time Gilbert noticed an extremely puzzled expression on his countenance. As they went upstairs to the

coffee-room, Major Braddock took advantage
of an opportunity to whisper to his nephew,
· "Deuced odd, Bertie, but I'll swear I have
seen your friend before."

"Not likely, I think," rejoined Slade.
" Some likeness probably misleads you."

"Not a bit of it," rejoined the Major,
testily. He had been hurried; his valet
had forgotten his buttonhole, and had to be
dispatched in a hansom cab in hot haste
in search of this indispensable adjunct at
nearly the last moment. Still mystified and
troubled in that mild way, in which not
being able to call a face to our recollection
does bother us, Major Braddock sat down to
his dinner. But the clear turtle was undeniable, and by the time the glass of
Madeira, its natural sequence, had been
swallowed, the Major dismissed the subject,
and had given himself up to enjoyment.
The dinner proved a success on every point.
The champagne was iced to a turn, the
claret was warmed to a nicety, and Charlie,

with the aid of the few hints he had received, had no difficulty in passing as, what
he really was, a genuine unaffected gentle-
manly young fellow. It was evident that
he had found favour in the Major's sight,
and when the quotation was dexterously
fired off, over a wonderous cunning *salmi*
that appeared as the dinner wore on, the
Major exclaimed,

"My dear young friend, allow me to con-
gratulate you. You have the making of an
epicure, and a considerable rudimentary
knowledge of the highest art and civilisa-
tion. I have little doubt that in of course
time you'll be as good a judge of a dinner
as I am!" And the Major uttered these
words in the same manner that another man
might have suggested a Victoria Cross or a
K.C.B.-ship as goals in a military career.
"It is to be regretted" continued the Major,
glancing sadly down at his own portly pro-
portions, "that the acquirement of such
knowledge does spoil the figure, but, as Mr.

Weller remarked, and he must (in his rough way) have been one of us, 'Width and wisdom go together.' "

After a couple of cigars Charlie, in obedience to a hint from his mentor, took his departure.

"He'll do, Bertie; he'll do! As nice a young one as I have seen for some time. I shall have great pleasure in doing all I can for him. I cannot think who his face reminds me of —— God bless my soul! I have it now!—being here recalls it to my memory. That is the young fellow I saw about a fortnight ago playing billiards in the next room with that old robber Dick Kynaston. And I'll tell you what, Bertie, my boy; if Devereux has got any money, the sooner you give him a hint the better. I know what Dick Kynaston can do on a billiard-table. And during the little time that I looked on he was playing with young Devereux as a cat plays with a mouse."

"I shouldn't think Charlie Devereux was

worth Kynaston's attention in that way.
Of course he knows them. They were up
hunting in his country all last season. But
I'm very glad you like young Devereux,
and hope now that you'll give him a lift."

"I will, I will! But don't say too much
about it, Bertie; for I don't want to disappoint him; and—it may not come off."

"Quite good enough, uncle Robert, to
know that you'll do your best. But I'll be
careful not to arouse undue expectations."

The next afternoon Gilbert wended his
way to Onslow Gardens to tell Lettie what
had been accomplished.

"Most satisfactory, I assure you, Miss
Devereux. Major Braddock was perfectly
satisfied with your brother, and pronounced
him a very nice youngster. Even the quotation was fired off with great dexterity. I
have done everything possible, and though,
of course, we can't be quite certain, yet I
have little doubt my uncle will obtain him
a nomination. The examination, of course,

is Charlie's affair, but I don't suppose that
will bother him much."

"Whether it bothers him or not, he must
pass it," rejoined Miss Devereux, laughing;
"even if I have to turn schoolmistress, and
hear him his lessons daily. However, I
have no fear about that. Charlie will work
hard enough, if it is wanted, with an object
in view. And now, do you really leave
London to-morrow?"

"Yes, leave is up, and I must return to
York. It is not a bad quarter, but no place
seems a good one when you want to be
somewhere else. By the way, you are very
intimate with the Kynastons, are you not?"

"Yes," rejoined Lettie. "That is, with
Mrs. Kynaston. I like her very much. She
is as bright as she is pretty, and can be so
excessively amusing."

"But," said Gilbert, "I gather you don't
care much for Major Kynaston?"

"No," said Lettie, "I'm sure I don't
know why not, for he has always been very

civil and polite to me. I have no doubt
I am quite wrong, but he always gives me
the idea of being so insincere."

"I fancy he rather bears that character,"
said Slade; "but what has become of Mrs.
Connop?"

"She is to come back for me, and take
me out driving, and is very nearly due
now," and Lettie glanced at the clock. "I
was so anxious to hear of Charlie's pros-
pects that I waited in to see him. As for
thanking you for the good news you brought,
I cannot sufficiently; but you do understand, Mr. Slade, how very grateful I am,
don't you?"

Lettie had risen from her chair, and very
handsome the girl looked in the excitement
of the moment, and very handsome the girl
looked with her cheeks slightly flushed, and
her grey eyes sparkling with pleasure. This
getting her brother into the army was an
object very near to her heart. She was of
a warm-hearted, impulsive disposition, and

very fond of Charlie, and was extremely gratified at the prospect of Charlie's becoming a dragoon. Gilbert was by no means blind to her attractions, and thought Miss Devereux had never looked so handsome as she did at this moment.

"You're making much of a very small service," he said; "and I'm quite ashamed at the wealth of gratitude by which it is repaid. Don't you know we all go upon the recruiting service sometimes? I can only trust in the future that you'll have no cause to shake your head, and pointing at me, say: 'There's the Sergeant Kite that trapped my brother.'"

"I have no fear of the result," rejoined Lettie. "But, happen what may, I will promise never to blame you for it; here is my hand on it."

Slade took the small palm which Lettie extended, and not only pressed it warmly, but detained it a trifle longer than there was any necessity for. The girl coloured slightly as he at last released it, and then exclaimed,

"I hear the carriage, and must run and get my bonnet on. You stay and tell my aunt all about it. I shall be down again in ten minutes."

Mrs. Connop was as much delighted as Lettie with the news, and full of anxiety to know when Charlie might expect his nomination. When did Gilbert think that Charlie would be gazetted? what regiment was he likely to be appointed to? and various questions of a like nature, which Mr. Slade had to plead his utter inability to answer. Then, in the expansiveness of her nature, she begged him to come and dine, and spend his last evening with them; but Lettie fortunately returned just in time to remind her that they themselves were engaged that evening. And Lettie felt rather put out that it should happen to be so. However, there was no help for it. So Gilbert made his adieus, supplemented with

a promise to be at Lincoln to witness Polestar's triumph in the autumn

"I shall be a very happy woman, my
dear," said Mrs. Connop, as the carriage
rolled away Park-wards, "if I see Charlie
a dragoon, and you engaged to be married
before the year's out."

"Nonsense, aunt," replied Lettie. "How
can you be so foolish?"

"Mr. Slade is a very good-looking man,
and, although I don't suppose he's at all
made up his mind yet, I doubt whether
he'd call the idea 'nonsense' exactly. At
all events Charlie's commission is an event
more than probable, you must admit."

"Much more probable than the other,
auntie dear," rejoined Lettie, as she turned
her face away.

"We shall see," said Mrs. Connop,
tersely.

CHAPTER XV.

ENTERED FOR THE ARMY.

" I DON'T exactly see your object, Dick; but, as you know, I'm not in the habit of bothering you about reasons. It is usually sufficient for me to know what you want without troubling my head about why you want it. I have been civil to this Mr. Furzedon, as you requested; and, if you think it worth while, could make up a small dinner for him. What he wants is obvious: the man is mad to push his way into London society; we are one of his stepping-stones. Of course I can help him, though I don't think much of him; but it is for you to decide whether it is worth our while."

"Never mind the dinner, Kate, and never mind the 'why.' I have a strong idea that Furzedon may be very useful to me before long. I made a mistake about him to start with, and thought that because he was young he was innocent. That young man was born the wrong side of forty, and one would have to get up early to teach him anything he don't know. Why, if I didn't detect him foxing at billiards with me! It isn't that I couldn't beat his head off, but the cheek of his thinking that he could impose on a man of my experience!" and the Major looked as Tennyson might do at receiving a hint from a provincial poetaster.

"I had nothing to do with that," rejoined Mrs. Kynaston quietly; "only remember, if I am civil to him and forward his views, it is because you desire it. And now, Dick, one word in earnest. I don't say you mean the boy any harm; but I do know you have imbued Charlie Devereux with the idea that he can beat you at billiards, and probably many other games."

"What the deuce is it to you if he should think so? I can scarcely suppose, my lady," he continued with a sneer, "that you have interested yourself in a boy like that!"

"You happen to be wrong, Dick," she said quietly. "I have, though not in the way you would insinuate; but mind, I'll not see that boy plundered. And while paying this compliment to your skill I will also point out that it is surely not worth your while."

"That is a thing, Kate, you will, perhaps, allow me to judge for myself. You will be good enough to bear in mind that I stand no interference with my plans."

"It is very rarely that I run counter to your wishes," rejoined Mrs. Kynaston; "but you know from past experience that when I am firmly resolved on a thing I can be every bit as obstinate as you. Charlie Devereux shall come to no harm at your hands if

I can prevent it. As for Mr. Furzedon, I'll not raise a finger in his behalf."

"You fool!" rejoined the Major. "Only that you are creating a storm in a teacup, I would soon show you that you have to obey orders; but I am not likely to harm Charlie Devereux, for the best of all possible reasons —the game would not pay for the candle. There is never any harm in ascertaining any man's form at any game he fancies himself at, and that young undergraduate thinks he can play billiards."

"Now we understand each other," said Mrs. Kynaston; "we will leave him, if you please, in that delusion. At all events, he shall not be rudely awakened at my hands."

"A good deal of talk about nothing, as usual," sneered the Major. "I shan't be at home either to lunch or dinner, so make your own arrangements," and, so saying, the Major put on his hat, and having looked in the glass, and given a last twirl to his moustache, took his departure.

Hawks speedily recognise hawks—in short, beasts of prey rarely fail to detect one another. The carnivora of humanity are swiftly aware of each other's presence. Just as amongst those outside the pale of the law there are cabalistic signs and a shibboleth not understanded by ordinary people, so amongst the higher vultures of society there is a recognition that takes but a short time to arrive at. The adventurer who has lived over half Europe very rapidly takes stock of his brothers, and Kynaston had already discovered that Ralph Furzedon was a very promising professor of his own line of business.

"Just the partner I want," thought the Major. "Has some capital, but wants introductions and opportunities. We might do great things together. He would be an apt pupil with my experience to guide him."

What had first opened Kynaston's eyes to the precociousness of his young friend had been

Furzedon's accurate information with regard to Turf matters. The old usurer, of whom, as a parent, that gentleman was so heartily ashamed, had Jewish blood in his veins, and an intimate acquaintance with the tribes generally, and especially with those in his own way of business. Now the Jews have been invariably mixed up in all sport at which money is to be made—from the prize-ring to the racecourse. I can't call to mind a Hebrew cricketer, but to the Turf and the Ring the Israelites have largely contributed, and the former sendeth the Gentile constantly to Shadrach for the means with which to appease Levy. Therefore racing secrets are rife amongst these people, and Furzedon was constantly permitted to share their knowledge; and the information he had thus been occasionally able to proffer the Major had given that gentleman a high opinion of his capacity.

Who lists the wind where it blows?

Who can tell what mischief a woman's

vanity and caprice may occasion when wounded and disappointed? But let that woman's love be not a caprice, but a serious passion, and it's odds, like other fires, it leaves ruins behind it ere it burns itself out. Mrs. Kynaston, still brooding over her fancy for Gilbert Slade, is a woman in whom the fire is already smouldering, with vanity already mortified, and, in spite of an outwardly easy-going manner, of a temper that will reck little of consequences should the flames break out

As for that hussar speeding northwards, he little dreams of his conquest, or of the coil he has left behind him. He is by no means blind to feminine beauty, and quite recognises that Mrs. Kynaston is fair to look upon, and it was quite possible that, had not a fairer in his eyes than she dawned simultaneously on the horizon, he might have become her devoted cavalier for a time; but as it is he thinks only of Lettie, and has well-nigh forgotten Mrs. Kynaston's existence, a circumstance which that lady has far too good an opinion of her own attractions to ever dream of. That Gilbert Slade was wavering in his allegiance she did think. She was accustomed to that, but with this difference, that the wavering was usually in her favour, and at some other woman's expense.

Gilbert Slade found the stream of life in the northern capital run somewhat sluggish after London. The quaint old city waxes somewhat drowsy in the dog-days, only to wake up again when August brings racing on the Knavesmire, and the Leger and the hunting-season are near at hand. However, Gilbert made the best of things, and was getting through what is rather the dead season in the country—to men—very fairly, wondering occasionally what Miss Devereux was doing, and whether she was still in town, when one morning the post brought him a letter from his uncle Robert, which necessitated his at once communicating with that young lady. It was dated from the " Thermopolium," and ran as follows:—

"DEAR BERTIE,—

"I have succeeded in getting a nomination for your *protégé*, and if he prospers he won't be the first soldier who has owed his success in his profession to the attractions of his female relations. His Royal Highness was exceedingly nice about it, and said, 'I can oblige you, Major Braddock, in what you want, and I shall have much pleasure in doing so. There is a cornetcy going in your old regiment, and I'm sure I can't do better for him than that. I inspected them not long ago, and found them, as usual, all that they ought to be. Leave his name and address in the outer room, and I'll see Mr. Devereux gets his nomination at once. There will be an examination in October, and he will be gazetted as soon as he has got through that,' and then His Royal Highness remarked, laughing, 'I was glad to find that the champagne of the ——th

Hussars was as good as ever; Colonel
Higginson told me that you still looked
after them in that respect, and are a sort
of honorary mess president even yet.' I
thanked His Highness, and told him I still
tried to do my duty to my country. And
so I do, you dog! Am I not always recom-
mending her defenders to drink the best
brands only? Nothing injures the constitution more than drinking bad wine. Now,
Master Bertie, I have succeeded in getting
young Devereux entered, bear in mind I
shan't like it if he's beat. Tell him he *must*
pass. I don't want His Royal Highness to
blow me up for having interfered in behalf
of a confounded fool. You had better write
to him at once, and tell him to look up his
books again. Thank goodness, in my time
they didn't think it necessary we should
know so much before we began. They
caught us young, and left it to the regiment
to break us.

" Your affectionate uncle,

ROBERT BRADDOCK."

Gilbert Slade was excessively pleased at the result of the Major's interference. He felt that he really had been of prompt service to Miss Devereux in this business. And then he thought that it would be rather a credit to himself to have introduced a recruit who could ride like Charlie into the regiment, for Gilbert had too much of the racing instincts of his family not to recognise that Charlie only wanted practice to become a really good gentleman rider, and even in a cavalry regiment men good between the flags are rare. There was one thing—it was of course imperative upon him now to write to Miss Devereux; and somehow he thought it would be rather pleasant to open a correspondence with Lettie. That missive duly arrived in Onslow Gardens, and threw the recipient and Mrs. Connop into a state of the wildest delight, tempered with no little anxiety on the subject of this examination. She had heard Charlie speak of men being plucked for their "little go," which she knew meant failure to pass an

examination of some sort; and her confidence in her brother's riding was considerably greater than that she reposed in
his reading. As for Mrs. Connop, she felt
quite confident of her favourite nephew's
ability to do anything in that way. Had he
not gone through a course of University
training? and was it likely that an examination for the army could have had any
terrors for a man who had undergone such
a preparation? But she, too, had her misgivings; it is often the case, we attain what
we ardently desire, and are immediately
afflicted with doubts as to whether, after
all, we were not, perhaps, better without it.
Charlie, she knew, although she knew it
very partially, had developed a faculty for
getting into money troubles at the University; and her experience told her that equal
facility and greater temptation existed for
indulging this infirmity in the army. And
it did occur to Mrs. Connop, even in this
hour of triumph, that his outfit might not

be the only demand that would be made upon her purse-strings.

Lettie hastened to reply to Gilbert Slade's letter, and thank him for the trouble he had taken in her brother's behalf. "Indeed, Mr. Slade," she said, "it has been very good of you to take all this trouble in Charlie's behalf. And I have no doubt that it was mainly the cunning hints he received from you which enabled him to make himself acceptable to Major Braddock, to whom also we feel very much indebted about the whole business. The idea of his being in the same regiment as yourself is delightful, because I am sure that you will put him in the way of things; and, though I have no fear of his soon making his way, yet the life will be strange to him at first, as he has had no experience of the ways of military men. As for passing, he writes very confidently, and vows 'that he shall pull through, though it may be with a fall or two;' and, as I know he is very much in earnest about obtaining his commission, I believe him. Once more, Mr. Slade, I must say that I don't know how to tell you how grateful we feel. You must come down and see Polestar win at Lincoln; and then, perhaps, we may induce you to come on to North Leach, and have a few days' hunting in the wolds. With kind regards from auntie,

"Yours most sincerely,

"LETTIE DEVEREUX."

Gilbert conceived this letter required acknowledgment, and wrote a courteous reply, in which he expressed his hope of assisting at Polestar's expected triumph in the autumn; and further requesting that he might be informed as speedily as possible of the result of the fray between Charlie and his torturers; but Miss Devereux made no further sign, and it was not till the end of September that he received a letter from Charlie himself:—

"DEAR SLADE," he began, "I have gone

through my ordeal, and, although not
formally apprised of it, feel sure that I have
passed. They put me on in about the
easiest chapter of all Cæsar's Commentaries,
one about which, if you know anything of
Latin at all, you couldn't go wrong in. The
whole examination, as it stands at present, is
a farce, and one which no ordinary schoolboy could possibly be plucked over, with
one exception; old Budgall, who examines
in history, has collected a bundle of very
dry facts, thickly studded with dates, which
he has published. He examines you chiefly
out of his own book, and dates are his
hobby. Of this I luckily got a hint, so just
struggled hard at his chronological table for
six weeks; deuced lucky I did so, for the
bigger half of my questions were of that
nature. I answered them like the well-
crammed gosling I was, and have very little
doubt that I shall have totally forgotten all
about them ere six months are over my
head. Never mind! they have served my

turn, and I shall hope to be with you at York this winter, and have a good time with the York and Ainsty. Good-bye, and no end of thanks for all you have ever done for me.

"Ever yours,

"CHARLIE DEVEREUX."

Army examinations, it must be borne in mind, were quite in their infancy when Mr. Devereux passed so triumphantly through the ordeal. They have become competitive since, and assumed a very different complexion; education, indeed, seems highly necessary for anything, except as a qualification for the electorate.

CHAPTER XVI.

DEAREST FRIENDS " MAY " DIFFER.

It was not till the very last week of her
London visit that Lettie received Slade's
letter containing the news of Charlie's nomination, and it was only when she wrote to
Kate Kynaston, proposing to call and say
" Good-bye," that lady learnt the fact that,
in the event of success, young Devereux was
to be gazetted to Gilbert's regiment. If she
had not been satisfied with Mr. Slade's interference in the matter before, her anger
about it now was tolerably pronounced.
She was not going to be out-manœuvred
by a chit of a country-girl like that, if she
knew it; and she persistently regarded

Gilbert as having fallen captive, metaphori-
cally speaking, to her own spear. She was
not likely to submit to having the spoils of
the chase wrested from her in this fashion.
Charlie in the same regiment, and naturally,
at his sister's bidding, perpetually bringing
Mr. Slade with him to North Leach! Had
Mrs. Kynaston been on the Board of Ex-
aminers I would not have given much for
Mr. Devereux's chance of passing, nor had
she been Colonel of the regiment do I think
much leave would have been accorded to
him just at present. On one point that
lady was more resolute than ever—that,
though he might escape from her thrall,
Gilbert should never be husband to Lettice
Devereux.

But outwardly her brow was as smooth
as of yore, and her congratulations to Lettie
on paper apparently warm and sincere.
Women, when the quarrel is à l'outrance,
know better than to betray themselves;
they bide their time, but when that comes

don't think they will spare their hand, or fail to send the steel home to its bitterest length. She turned over in her mind how this union might be prevented: there was plenty of time—it was a thing that might never come about, and, even should she learn that the pair were engaged, it was very possible, thought Mrs. Kynaston, to arrange a slip 'twixt that cup and lip. Marriages may be made in Heaven, perhaps, but that they are frequently ruptured on earth, both in the egg and when full-grown, we have much demonstration of, and how often woman's jealousy or man's frailty contributes to such sad ending, what philosopher shall determine? But I fancy the former has shattered as much matrimonial happiness as can be attributed to any enemy of Hymen.

Suddenly it flashed vaguely before Mrs. Kynaston's mind that this new *protégé* of her husband—Mr. Furzedon—might be a useful card in her hand in the game she contemplated playing. She had read that gentleman's character pretty correctly considering the little she had seen of him. She knew that he was selfish, had a strong suspicion that he was niggardly, but she further knew for certain that his great ambition was to obtain some social status in the great London world. He admired Miss Devereux —that was a fact patent to any one gifted with the power of perception—but Mr. Furzedon was not a man likely to marry, except deliberately, and in furtherance of the line he had chalked out for himself.

"It would not be such a hard thing," mused Mrs. Kynaston, "to make Furzedon anxious to marry Lettie Devereux. Her brother getting into a crack dragoon regiment is one step towards it! Let Mr. Furzedon only be persuaded that Miss Devereux is an acknowledged beauty, whose face is a passport to fashion's portals, and he will be keen enough to woo her. He would prefer a wife with money, perhaps—

with a handle to her name, undoubtedly— but he is far too shrewd a judge not to know that a man with no antecedents and only a moderate command of money cannot expect the pick of the matrimonial market. Yes," continued Mrs. Kynaston, still following up the same train of thought, "it is quite possible that Mr. Furzedon may be a very useful card to me in future. I don't like the man myself, nor do I suppose that Dick does either, for, to do him justice, although necessity compels him to know very electro-plated gentlemen at times, poor old Dick thoroughly understands good form when he meets it. I usually obey my lord and master, and for once his wishes and mine conform. He has his reasons for wishing me to be civil to Mr. Furzedon; I also have mine. That slightly underbred young man promises to be rather a tame cat about our establishment;" and then Mrs. Kynaston, glancing at the clock, muttered softly to herself, "Lettie, my dear,

it is time you made your appearance. How
pleased I shall be to see you! How sad I
shall be that we are about to part! And
how sad, my love, I am at the thought that
I cannot bite you! "

She had not to wait long. A few minutes
more and Miss Devereux was announced,
and Mrs. Kyraston rose and received her
with the greatest effusion.

" I am rather late, I know," said Lettie,
as she sank into an easy chair, "but there is
always so much to do the last few days;
people whom one has almost forgot have to
be called on, and people whom you had hoped
had forgot all about you suddenly turn up
and pay visits of unwarrantable length and
never-to-be-forgotten dreariness. I don't
know how it is, but these latter people
always circumvent the servants; your dearest friends may be turned away from the
door, but, whatever the instructions, these
people invariably at least gain the drawing-

room, and you are very lucky if they don't catch you in it."

" Yes," replied Mrs. Kynaston, gaily, " few people possess such a treasure as Staples. He was with the Major before I married. He is a little brusque in his manner, I grant, but he has almost an un-erring instinct of whom to let in and whom to keep out. He has a capital memory, and the slightest hint suffices him. Dick always says, in joke, that there are times when Staples will say ' Not at home ' to *him*, and that nothing but his latchkey makes admis-sion to his own house a certainty. Un-doubtedly Staples is a very superior watch-dog. As for the importunate creditor— don't look shocked, Lettie, half the West End of London are troubled in this wise— Staples recognises them, I verily believe, by their knock, let them play such salvo as they will upon our door; while the vague-ness of his knowledge as to whether Major

Kynaston is in town, or ever will be in town
again, is simply unsurpassable."

"An invaluable man, Staples," rejoined
Lettie. " I must consider myself fortunate
to be in his good graces."

" Oh, yes; he knows you, and that you
are one of the privileged; but I haven't
congratulated you. I am so pleased about
Charlie, and how very nice it is that he
should have got into Mr. Slade's regiment.
It will be especially nice for you, my dear ! "
continued Mrs. Kynaston, archly.

" Why so ? " asked Lettie.

" Oh, I don't know," said Mrs. Kynaston,
carelessly. " Still, it's always convenient to
have one's brothers and admirers in the
same bundle. When you want a few young
men for a ball you will always be able to
write to Charlie to come, and to bring two
or three brother-officers with him. And if
you haven't, after the first twelve months,
taught him *whom* to bring, then you deserve
to die an old maid."

" How can you say such things?" cried Lettie, hotly. " My brothers have always been accustomed to bring such friends as they like to North Leach, and it is not likely that Charlie, when he becomes a dragoon, will renounce that privilege—why should he? and why should not one of those friends be Mr. Slade? He, at all events, has a strong claim on our hospitality, if only for the service he has just rendered us."

" Quite so, my dear," assented her companion. " Men have done more than that for the love of *les beaux yeux*, and received far less guerdon than, I prophesy, will be Mr. Slade's lot. Now, don't get angry, Lettice, but, bear in mind, these soldiers are arrant flirts—they woo, and they ride away. Don't let your heart out of your keeping till the engagement ring is on your finger."

" What nonsense you are talking!" rejoined Lettie, petulantly. " Mr. Slade has

undeniably been very kind in this business
to Charlie. I presume I may feel grateful
to him without having the slightest ulterior
thought ? "

"Of course you may," rejoined Mrs. Kynaston, with a sarcastic little smile ; " but
you wouldn't be a woman if you hadn't one.
What do you suppose made Mr. Slade take
such interest in Charlie. Pooh ! Lettie,
don't juggle with facts ; nor attempt to
hoodwink a woman of the world like me.
If it was not from admiration of yourself, I
would simply know why did he trouble his
head about Charlie ? "

Lettie flushed, and felt very uncomfortable under the merciless railliery of her
hostess. She most devoutly wished herself
well out of Chester Street, and that she had
never come to bid Mrs. Kynaston good-bye.
She was quite conscious that there was a
good deal of truth in what her hostess had
said. She was not yet quite in love with
Gilbert Slade ; but she did not disguise from

herself that she was in a very fair way to become so. And all these semi-jeering remarks of Mrs. Kynaston's stung like so many pin-pricks; but, sharp as the stab may be, no Indian brave ever stands torture with more assumed indifference than a woman in society endures the gibes of her sisters.

"I can hardly answer that question," Miss Devereux replied at length. "My experience, of course, does not go so far as yours by some years, but I have known people do kindly actions without seeking much gain for themselves. You know best; but don't you think it would be rather a dreary world if we never did our neighbour a good turn without calculation? Surely, Kate, you don't look to be paid in kind for every small assistance you may render your fellow-creatures in this world?"

"I usually am," replied that lady, with asperity. "'As we sow, so shall we reap,' so say the Scriptures—a truth that know-

ledge of the world tells me may be read
in very different lights. The kindnesses
you have sown generally produce but a
crop of ingratitude. Be a good friend to
a man, and he drops you for the first face
that catches his fancy; be a good friend to
a woman, and she devotes every art she possesses to steal from you your lover or your
husband. Don't look so ' mazed,' Lettie!
You were kind enough to remind me of my
many years' additional experience, and *that*
is the outcome of them."

If Miss Devereux was young, she was no
fool: she was vaguely conscious that some
jealousy concerning Gilbert Slade was at
the bottom of Mrs. Kynaston's bitterness;
but she had never grasped, nor was it likely
she ever would, that that lady had considered the hussar her own peculiar property, and, as has been said before, this was
a conclusion on Mrs. Kynaston's part that
circumstances by no means warranted.

There is no helping these things; men go

on telling stories till they arrive at the belief that they were *bonâ fide* the heroes of them. Men regard property that may come to them very often as property that must come to them, and eventually as property that actually belongs to them. When the holder dies, and his will announces that the late proprietor has taken a different view of things, such men are simply crushed with a sense of injustice, and that they have been the victims of heartless robbery.

"I don't know what makes you speak so bitterly to-day, but I suppose you are in low spirits ; something has gone wrong, perhaps, and then, we all know, life looks none so rosy. I can't plead guilty to knowing much about that sort of thing; but even a schoolgirl has occasional fits of depression : her music gets the best of her, or she's baulked in some expected pleasure. I thought you would be so glad to hear of Charlie's good fortune."

"So I am, of course ; haven't I told you

so ? And how nice you will find it having him in a crack Hussar regiment."

Miss Devereux did not reply immediately —there is more than one way of offering congratulations, and Lettie was quite conscious that there was a flavour of hyssop about those of Mrs. Kynaston. "Well, good-bye," she said, rising ; "I do hope you will think better of it, and take The Firs again for next season. We shall miss you and the Major sadly as neighbours; and remember that the advantages which you have just said will accrue to me from Charlie's commission will also tend to make our few balls still more lively for you; in short," concluded Lettie with a laugh, "if we can muster a few young men at North Leach, it is good for the whole neighbourhood in that way."

"Good-bye," said Mrs. Kynaston, as she shook hands with her again. "I don't know at all as yet if The Firs is destined to be our winter quarters this year. One

piece of advice, my dear, at parting : don't
be too philanthropic, nor too ready to part
with the partners your brother has delivered
into your hand.   You are very pretty,
Lettie ; but men are very fanciful, and let
the bell-wether take up with a Gorgon, and
the rest of them are struggling madly to
secure her hand for the next dance."

Miss Devereux made no response. She
was, indeed, only too glad to bring her visit
to a termination. She was quite conscious
that their conversation, though nominally
friendly, had been "on the jar" throughout,
and that Mrs. Kynaston's congratulations
had been very far from cordial ; she did not
understand it. She had thought that lady
really fond of them all, and that she would
have been delighted at hearing of Charlie's
good fortune. But she felt quite sure that
there was something in his appointment to
the ——th Hussars that did not meet Mrs.
Kynaston's approval. Then as Miss Devereux drove back to Onslow Gardens her

thoughts reverted to Mrs. Kynaston's innu-
endo, that when Charlie had joined his
regiment there would be much facility for
asking Mr. Slade to come down with him to
North Leach. She wondered if Mr. Slade
would care to pay such a visit. She wondered a little as to whether he cared for
her. She had good evidence that he had
not forgotten her, or he would hardly have
taken all this trouble in Charlie's behalf.
"Ah," thought Lettie, "how jolly it would
be if Polestar should win at Lincoln, and
they all come back to North Leach to have
two or three days' hunting, and celebrate
his triumph." And in *they* I fancy Mr.
Gilbert Slade was emphatically included.

WESTMINSTER:

PRINTED BY NICHOLS AND SONS,

25, PARLIAMENT STREET.

www.ingramcontent.com/pod-product-compliance
Lightning Source LLC
Chambersburg PA
CBHW030623030726
47497CB00006B/1610